Jidi Majia

吉狄马加

彝族，1961年6月生于中国西南部最大的彝族聚居区凉山彝族自治州，是中国当代最具代表性的诗人之一，同时也是一位在国际上具有广泛影响的诗人，其诗歌已被翻译成三十多种文字，在世界几十个国家出版了六十余种版本的翻译诗集。曾获中国第三届新诗（诗集）奖、郭沫若文学奖荣誉奖、庄重文文学奖、肖洛霍夫文学纪念奖、柔刚诗歌荣誉奖、国际华人诗人笔会中国诗魂奖、南非姆基瓦人道主义奖、欧洲诗歌与艺术荷马奖、罗马尼亚《当代人》杂志卓越诗歌奖、布加勒斯特城市诗歌奖、波兰雅尼茨基文学奖、英国剑桥大学国王学院银柳叶诗歌终身成就奖、波兰塔德乌什·米钦斯基表现主义凤凰奖。创办青海湖国际诗歌节、青海国际诗人帐篷圆桌会议、凉山西昌邛海国际诗歌周以及成都国际诗歌周。现任中国作家协会副主席、书记处书记。

Jidi Majia, a native of Yi ethnic minority, was born in June 1961 in the Liangshan Yi Autonomous Prefecture, in the southwest of China. As one of the most representative poets in China,attaining an international reputation, Jidi Majia's poems have been published in dozens of countries and regions,having been translated into over 30 languages. He has been awarded the Third China Poetry Prize, Guo Moruo Literature Prize, Zhuang Zhongwen Literary Prize, Sholokhov Memorial Prize, Rou Gang Literary Prize, the "China Poetic Spirit Award" of International Chinese P. E. N., the Mkiva International Humanitarian Award of South Africa, the 2016 European Poetry and Art Homer Award, the Poetry Prize awarded by the Romanian magazine *Contemporary People*, the 2017 Bucharest Poetry Prize, the 2017 Ianicius Prize of Poland, and Lifetime Achievement Award of Xu Zhimo Poetry Prize of Cambridge and Tadeusz Miciński "PHONENIX" International Expressionistic Award of Poland. Since 2007, he has founded a series of poetry events including Qinghai Lake International Poetry Festival, Qinghai Intl. Poets Tent Forum, Xichang Qionghai Poets Week and Chengdu International Poetry Week. He currently serves as the Vice President of China Writers Association.

Denis Mair

梅丹理

梅丹理(Denis Mair)，美国诗人，中英文翻译者，俄亥俄州立大学中文硕士。曾担任美国宾夕法尼亚州立大学东亚语文系讲师，现任北京中坤基金翻译顾问。吉狄马加诗歌的主要翻译者。译作包括真华法师的《参学琐谈》(纽约州立大学出版社, 1992)、冯友兰的《三松堂自序》(夏威夷大学出版社, 2000)、朱朱的《一幅画的诞生》(新星出版社)。诗歌翻译包括奚密、马悦然编的《台湾新诗选》(哥伦比亚大学出版社, 2005)，杨四平编的《当代中文诗歌选》(上海文艺出版社, 2007)，《阎志的诗》(Homa & Sekey Books, 2012)，吉狄马加的《黑色狂欢曲》(俄克拉何马大学出版社, 2014)，吉狄马加的《群山的影子》(南非姆基瓦出版社, 2014)，吉狄马加的《从雪豹到马雅科夫斯基》(Kallatumba Press, 2017)，杨克的《地球苹果的两半》(俄克拉何马大学出版社, 2017)。他翻译的当代诗人还包括严力、孟浪等。其个人英文诗集《木刻里的人》于2004年由洛杉矶Valley Contemporary Poets出版。

Denis Mair, an American poet, holds an M.A. in Chinese from Ohio State University and has taught as lecturer at the Pennsylvania State University. He is currently translation consultant for Zhongkun Cultural Fund, Beijing; he also serves as translator for Jidi Majia. Denis translated books by the Buddhist monk Shih Chen-hua (SUNY Albany Press, 1992), the philosopher Feng Youlan (Hawaii University Press, 2000), and the art critic Zhu Zhu (New Star Press, 2009). His poetry translations include: Ximi, Ma Yueran, *Frontier Taiwan* (Columbia University Press, 2005); Yang Siping, *Contemporary Chinese Poetry* (Shanghai Literary Arts Press, 2007); Yan Zhi, *Reading the Times* (Homa & Sekey Books, 2012); Jidi Majia, *Rhapsody in Black* (Univ. of Oklahoma, 2014); Jidi Majia, *Shade of Our Mountain Range* (Mkhiva Foundation, 2014); Jidi Majia, *From the Snow Leopard to Mayakovsky* (Kallatumba Press, 2017); as well as Yang Ke, *Two Halves of the World Apple* (Univ. of Oklahoma Press, 2017), etc. He has also translated poetry by Yan Li, Meng Lang and many others. His own poetry collection *Man Cut in Wood* was published by Valley Contemporary Poets (Los Angeles, 2004).

支持单位：中国野生动物保护协会
Supported by: China Wildlife Conservation Association

作者手稿
珍贵影像
中英双语版

我，
雪豹

吉狄马加
著

梅丹理
译

自然影像中国
供图

The Author's Manuscripts
Precious Images
In both Chinese and English

I,
Snow
Leopard

Jidi Majia
Translated by Denis Mair

Photos provided by
Nature Image China

河南科学技术出版社
·郑州·

序

［美］巴里·洛佩兹 作　曹明伦 译

在《我，雪豹……》一诗中，诗人吉狄马加邀请我们去听雪豹的声音。我们从一开始就知道，这种动物并非西方科学所定义的雪豹。它是一种有精神生活的生物，一种具有人格特征的生物。如果要我们设法为这种声音定位，它可以被描述为一名睿智的守护者的声音，一个体现其文化历史和崇高价值的人的声音。

我们在这首诗中听到的声音，发自一位生活严肃、淡泊名利的智者。从其知性和感性来看，这声音是传统的，也是现代的。

那声音听起来急迫，但并不惊慌。那声音在恳求，但不是乞求。那声音中既无多愁善感，也没有冷嘲热讽。那声音在向我们呼唤，从一个暌违已久的时代，从一个世人更博雅的时代，从一个头顶天空未被地狱之彩映红的时代。

吉狄马加是一位彝族诗人。他自己就诞生于一种传统文化，一种在历史的长河中形成于青藏高原东侧边缘地区的文化。他选择要我们去聆听一头雪豹，这本身就具有非凡的意义。诗中有一个戏剧性的场景：烟灰色兽皮，镶着“幻化成的”玫瑰形暗花图案，又粗又长的兽尾——越崖纵壁时的平衡杆——还有灰绿色的凝视。一种既有隐喻分量又有生物凭证的动物，一个濒于灭绝的物种，被心怀恶意的天空遮暗。显而易见，吉狄马加是从一个特殊的地理位置给我们讲他的预言，但那不是一个限定的位置，不是一个有疆界的地区。我们不难想象我们自己就在那个地方，我们也能感觉到那头雪豹想告诉我们的超凡智慧，以及它对全世界的呼吁。

从青藏高原的山顶居所，俯瞰远方山谷中淡蓝色的积雪，然后仰望它领地上方的无垠星空，我们终于明白，实际上，那头雪豹所告诉我们的，我们几乎都早已了然于胸。然而，它的意图并非要带给我们超凡的智慧。凭它对悠远时间的理解，凭它对浩渺空间的领悟，它的目的是要延续人类习俗礼仪复兴的使命。它要让我们记住我们每个人都倾向于遗忘的东西。我们总习惯性地忘却我们想要我们的生命体现出的意义。毋庸置疑，借重述根植于世界上各种文化中的原始故事，这首诗提醒我们别忘了人类意识的致命弱点——记忆的衰减甚至湮灭。我们屡屡忽略我们想要我们的生命象征的意义。为了保护我们，年长者必须持续不断地让我们重新熟悉我们的理想。

吉狄马加的雪豹是一名“山地的水手”，是偏远地区的一尊“保护神”。与我们多数人不同，那头雪豹眼中的时间呈“液态”。它能听见飘到它跟前的“微尘的声音”。它是“雷鸣后的寂静”。它是“地震的战栗”和一股“离心力”。最重要的是，它发现其天然位置在一个玄幻之境，在黑暗与光明间穿梭，在生命与死亡间游走，在每一对二元对立的事物间交错。

那头雪豹说，它正试图在我们心中唤醒另一种语言，另一种解决我们所面临的全球困境的方式。它念出的“祈祷词”是“为这一片大地上的所有生灵”。面对“危机四伏的世界”，它说“我们大家都已无路可逃”——而无路可逃者包括濒临灭绝的雪豹和它们猎食的旱獭，包括任何贬低其他部族的部族，包括那些为了更舒适的生活而盲目毁坏这个星球的世人，包括压迫者和被压迫者。一个生灵的命运就是另一个生灵的命运。

PREFACE

by Barry Lopez to Jidi Majia's *I, Snow Leopard...*

In Jidi Majia's poem *I, Snow Leopard...*, Jidi Majia asks us to listen to the voice of the snow leopard, an animal we know right from the start is not the *Panthera unica* of Western science. It is a being with an interior life, with the attributes of personhood. Its voice, were we to try to place it, could be described as that of a wisdom keeper.

The voice we hear in the poem is the expression of someone who takes life seriously but who has no cloying desire to be known or accepted. The voice is traditional, but also modern in its awareness and sensibility.

The voice is urgent but not panicked. It is imploring but not begging. It is without sentimentality or irony. And it calls to us from an unremembered time, an era when people knew better, when the sky above was not inflamed with the colors of Hell.

It makes eminent sense that the Nuosu (Yi) poet Jidi Majia, himself born into a traditional culture, one that came to life over time on the northeastern edge of the Tibetan plateau, would choose to have us listen to a snow leopard. Here is a dramatic presence: the smoke-gray fur, chased with a pattern of dark rosettes "spun from the void," the long, heavy tail, its balance pole as it bounds across a cliff face, the pale green stare. An animal possessing both metaphorical weight and biological authority, an endangered species, shadowed by a malevolent sky. Majia's oracle speaks to us from a specific, local geography, clearly; but it isn't a restrictive geography, a circumscribed country. We can quite easily imagine ourselves in this place; we also feel the transcendence of the wisdom the snow leopard wishes to impart to us, its universal appeal.

From an eyrie on the Tibetan plateau, gazing down at blue-tinged snow in a mountain-girt valley far below, then up at unbounded star fields in his domain's night canopy, the snow leopard, it turns out, actually tells us little that we do not already know. His purpose, however, is not to bring us unprecedented wisdom. With his awareness of deep time and his appreciation of the vastness of earthly spaces, his intention is to continue the revitalizing work of human ceremony. He is reminding us of what every one of us is prone to forget. We regularly forget what we want our lives to mean. Indeed, the poem, in imitation of origin stories embedded in cultures the world over, is a reminder of the Achilles heel of human consciousness, the lapse and disintegration of memory. We repeatedly lose touch with what we intend our lives to stand for. To protect us, the elders must constantly reacquaint us with our ideals.

Majia's Snow Leopard is a "sailor of high terrain," a "guardian deity." Unlike most of us, the Snow Leopard sees time "in a liquid state." He can hear "the sound of a dust mote" drifting before him. He is "the stillness after lightning." He is "an earthquake tremor" and a "decentering force." Above all, he finds his natural place in the hazy ecotones between darkness and light, between death and birth, in the in-between of every opposing dyad.

The Snow Leopard says that he is trying to awaken in us another language, another way to address our now universal predicament. The "prayer" he prays is "for all creatures on this land." In acknowledging the "lurking dangers of our world," he says that "there is no escape route for any of us" — for endangered snow leopards or the marmots they hunt, for any tribe seeking to diminish another, for people mindlessly destroying the planet to make the world more comfortable for humans, for either the oppressors or the oppressed. The destiny of one is the destiny of the other.

吉狄马加

我，雪豹……

1

流星划过的时候
我的身体，在瞬间
被光明点燃，我的皮毛
燃烧如白雪的火焰

1

As a meteor parts the sky overhead
My body, in an instant
Is touched by radiance
Set alight in snow-white flames

1

流星划过的时候
我的身体，在瞬间
被光明烛照，我的皮毛
燃烧如白雪的火焰

我的影子，闪动成光的箭矢
犹如一条银色的鱼
消失在黑暗的苍穹
我是雪山真正的儿子
守望孤独，穿越了所有的时空
潜伏在岩石坚硬的波浪之间

And my shape is a lightning streak
Like a silvery fish receding
Against the dark vault of sky
I am the true son of snowy mountains
Watching over solitude, persisting
Through all temporal stages
Crouched among hardened waves of boulders

我的影子，闪动成光的箭矢
犹如一条银色的鱼
消失在黑暗的苍穹
我是雪山真正的儿子
守望孤独，穿越了所有的时空
潜伏在岩石坚硬的波浪之间

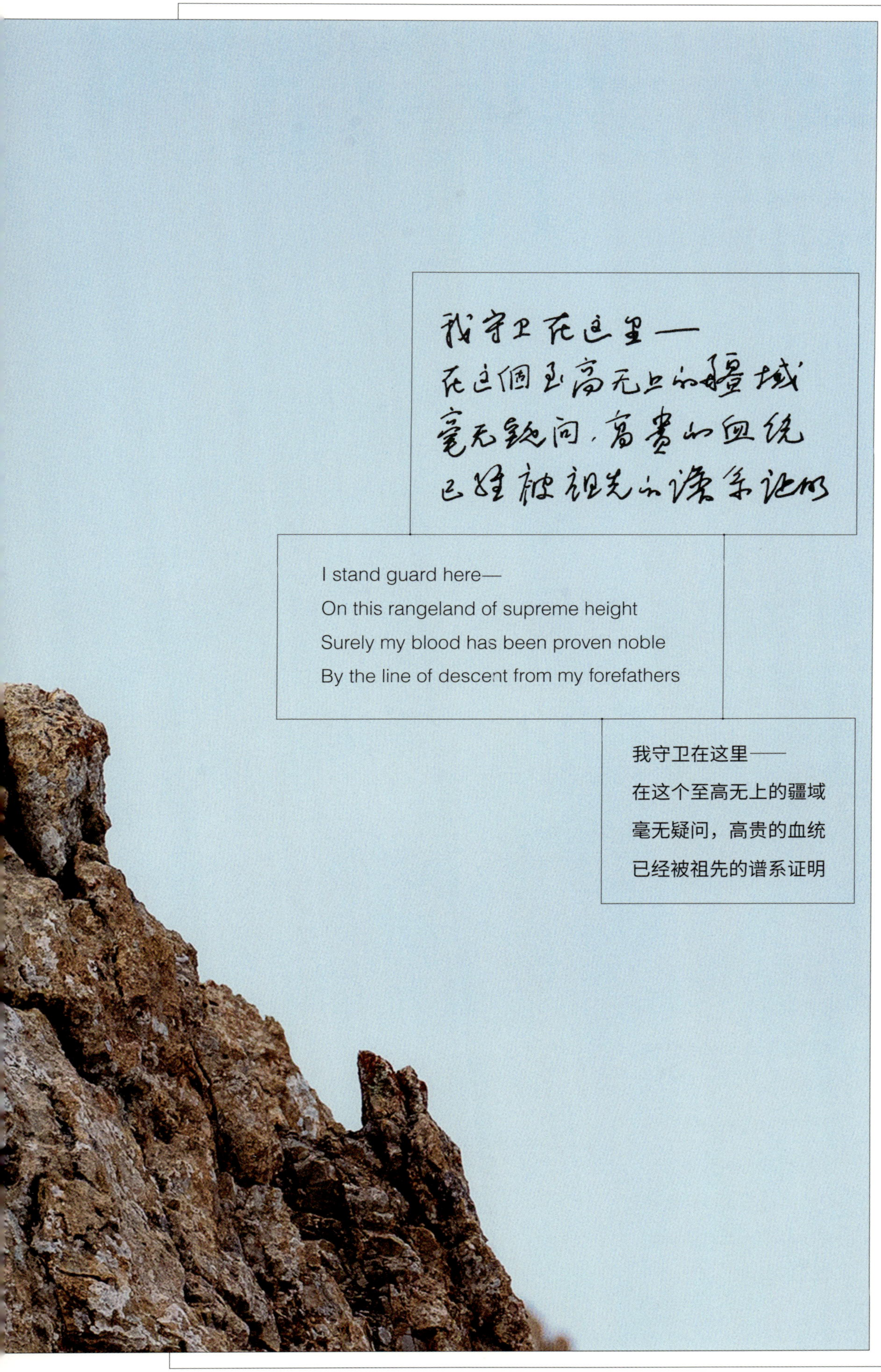

我守卫在这里——
在这個至高无上的疆域
毫无疑问，高贵的血统
已经被祖先的谱系证明

I stand guard here—
On this rangeland of supreme height
Surely my blood has been proven noble
By the line of descent from my forefathers

我守卫在这里——
在这个至高无上的疆域
毫无疑问，高贵的血统
已经被祖先的谱系证明

我的诞生——
是白雪千年孕育的奇迹
我的死亡——
是白雪轮回永恒的寂静
因为我的名字的含义：
我隐藏在雾和霭的最深处
我穿行于生命意识中的
另一個边缘

My birth was a miracle
Gestated for millennia in white snow
My death is cyclic transformation
Of silence in this snowy domain
Just as my name implies
I hide in mist and windborne frost
I too walk in awareness of life
But skirting its other margin

我的诞生——
是白雪千年孕育的奇迹
我的死亡——
是白雪轮回永恒的寂静
因为我的名字的含义：
我隐藏在雾和霭的最深处
我穿行于生命意识中的
另一个边缘

我的眼睛底部
绽放着呼吸的星光
我思想的珍珠
凝聚成黎明的水滴

Blooming from deep in my eyes
Is the starry glint of breath
The pearls of my thought
Coalesce into droplets of dawn

我的眼睛底部
绽放着呼吸的星光
我思想的珍珠
凝聚成黎明的水滴

我不是一段经文
刚开始的那个部分
我的声音是群山
战胜时间的沉默

In a long chapter of scripture
I am not the opening lines
Ranged mountains defeat time by silence
Which is also my voice

我不是一段经文
刚开始的那个部分
我的声音是群山
战胜时间的沉默

我不属于语言在天空
悬垂着的文字
我仅仅是一道光
留下闪闪发亮的纹路

I do not belong to those written words
Suspended by language from the sky
I am merely a beam of light
That leaves a radiant tracery

我不属于语言在天空
悬垂着的文字
我仅仅是一道光
留下闪闪发亮的纹路

我忠诚谎言
不会被情报的词语书写
我永远活在
虚无编织的界限之外
我不会选择离开
即便雪山已经死亡

I faithfully vow
No traitorous words will ever inscribe me
I forever live beyond boundaries
That some would fashion without substance
I will never choose to leave here
Even when death claims these snowy peaks

我忠诚诺言
不会被背叛的词语书写
我永远活在
虚无编织的界限之外
我不会选择离开
即便雪山已经死亡

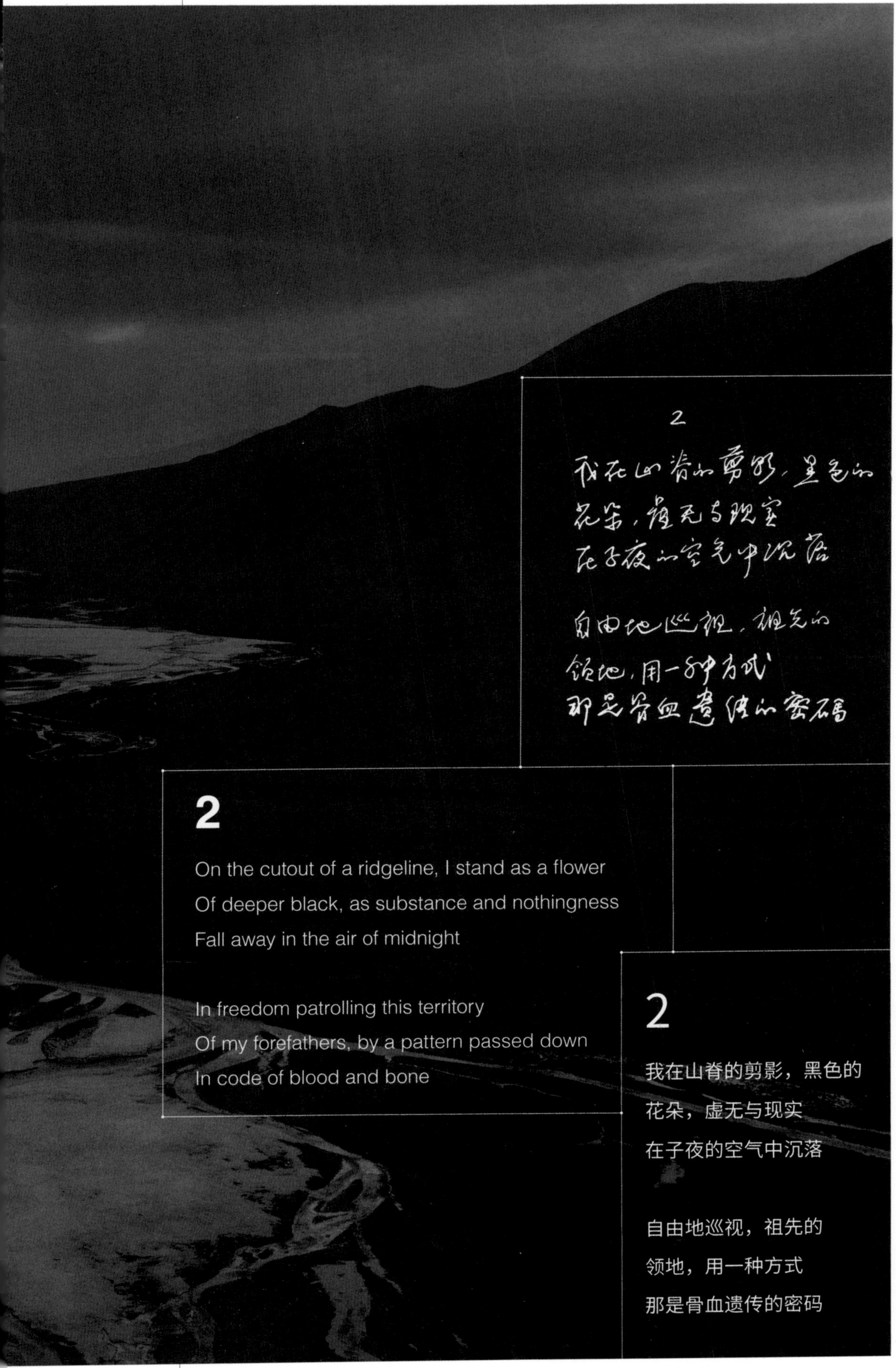

2

我在山脊的剪影，黑色的
花朵，虚无与现实
在子夜的空气中沉落

自由地巡视，祖先的
领地，用一种方式
那是骨血遗传的密码

2

On the cutout of a ridgeline, I stand as a flower
Of deeper black, as substance and nothingness
Fall away in the air of midnight

In freedom patrolling this territory
Of my forefathers, by a pattern passed down
In code of blood and bone

2

我在山脊的剪影，黑色的
花朵，虚无与现实
在子夜的空气中沉落

自由地巡视，祖先的
领地，用一种方式
那是骨血遗传的密码

在晨昏的时光，欲望
就会把我召唤
穿行在隐秘的沉默中

只有在这样的时刻
我才会去，真正重温
那个失去的时代……

In glimmering pre-dawn hours
Heeding the call of appetite
I wend my silent, secret way

Only in such moments
Do I truly bring alive
An epoch that seemed to have passed...

在晨昏的时光，欲望
就会把我召唤
穿行在隐秘的沉默之中

只有在这样的时刻
我才会去，真正重温
那个失去的时代……

3

望着坠落的星星
身体漂浮在宇宙的海洋
幽蓝的日光，伴随着
纯金的灵魂，正朝着
永无止境的方向上升

3

Watching a falling star
This body drifts in a cosmic sea
Eye-glint of ghostly blue keeps company
With a weightless soul, as they ascend
Toward ever-higher levels

3

望着坠落的星星
身体漂浮在宇宙的海洋
幽蓝的目光，伴随着
失重的灵魂，正朝着
永无止境的方向上升

还没有开始——
闪电般地纵身一跃
完满了悬崖的脚趾
已经卷着全身，和空气
谁也看不见，这样一个过程
我的呼吸、回忆、秘密的气息
已经全部覆盖了这片荒野
但不要寻找我，而是早已消失……

Before the body even starts
To clear the ground with lightning leap
Those legs filled with tensile strength
Strike up a beat on metallic air
In a series of movements no one sees
My breath and memories and secret scent
By now cover this wilderness, but do not seek me
Where all traces of masks are gone

还没有开始——
闪电般地纵身一跃
充满强度的脚趾
已敲击着金属的空气
谁也看不见，这样一个过程
我的呼吸、回忆、秘密的气息
已经全部覆盖了这片荒野
但不要寻找我，面具早已消失……

4

此时，我就是这片雪域
从吹过的风中，我聆听到
我骨骼发出的声响
一只鹰翻腾着，在与看不见的
对手搏击，那是我的影子
在光明和黑暗的
缓冲地带游离

4

Now, I myself am none other than this snowy realm
Move quietly and listen into the wind
You may hear the crack of my joints stretching
An eagle riding updrafts does combat
With an unseen rival—that is my shadow
Which ranges over the threshold zone
Between light and darkness
Where a valley meets with a river's course

4

此时，我就是这片雪域
从吹过的风中，能聆听到
我骨骼发出的声响
一只鹰翻腾着，在与看不见的
对手搏击，那是我的影子
在光明和黑暗的
缓冲地带游离

陨石鸟无声地降落
在那山谷和河流的交汇处
是我脚下的暗示和符号
如果一只旱獭
拼命地奔跑，但身后
都是不可见的追击

No bird of prey makes its silent plunge
I have left this as a sign for you to read
If a marmot scrambles for cover
Even where no pursuer
Is seen running behind it

没有鸟无声地降落
在那山谷和河流的交汇处
是我留下的暗示和符号
如果一只旱獭
拼命地奔跑，但身后
却看不见任何追击

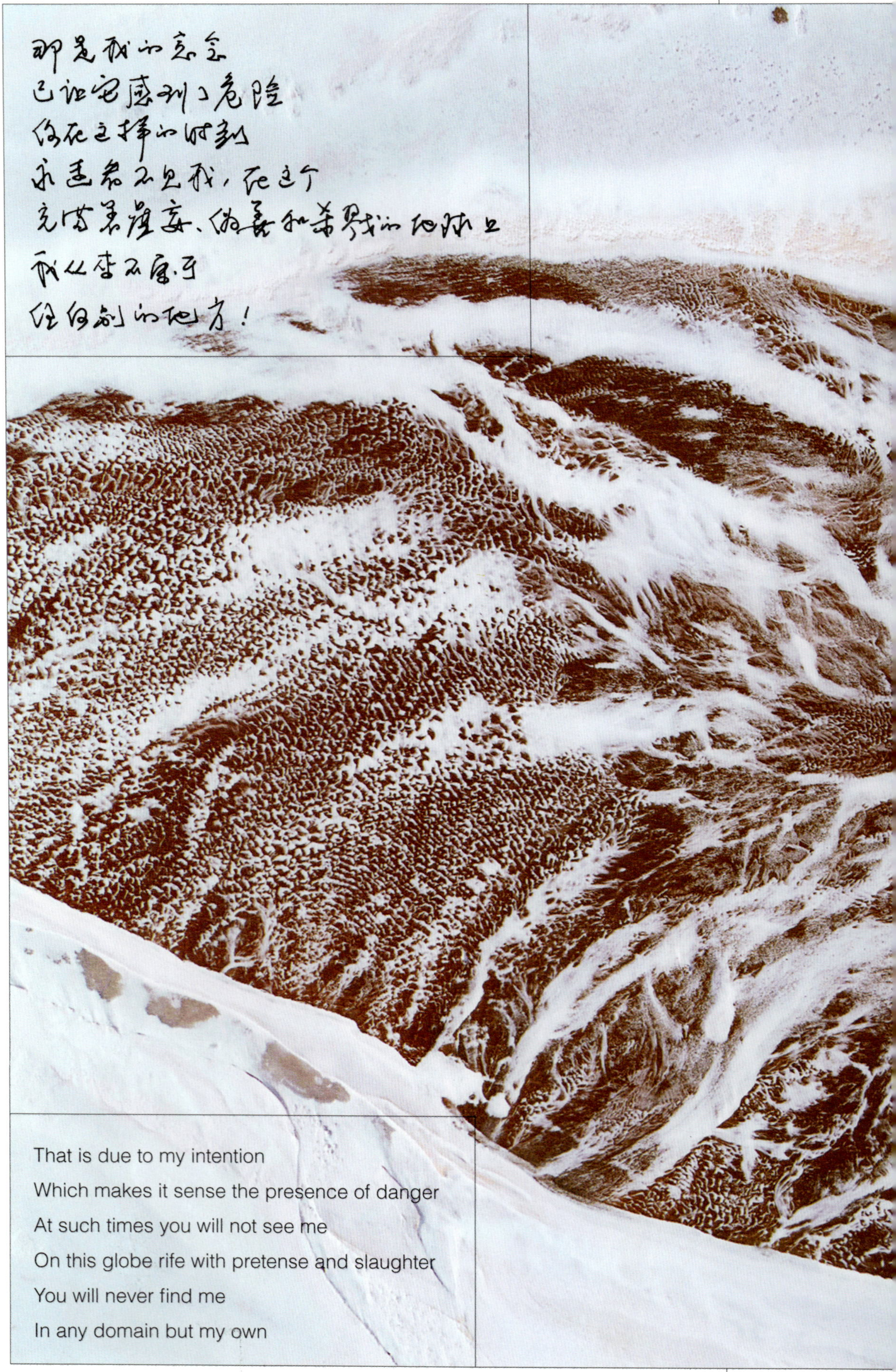

那是我的意念
已让它感到了危险
你在这样的时刻
永远看不见我，在这个
充满着虚妄、伪善和杀戮的地球上
我从来不属于
任何别的地方！

That is due to my intention
Which makes it sense the presence of danger
At such times you will not see me
On this globe rife with pretense and slaughter
You will never find me
In any domain but my own

那是我的意念
已让它感到了危险
你在这样的时刻
永远看不见我，在这个
充满着虚妄、伪善和杀戮的地球上
我从来不属于
任何别的地方！

5

我说不出所有
动物和植物的名字
但这却是一个圆形的世界
我不知道关于生命的天平
应该是，更靠左边一点
还是更靠右边一点，我只是
一只雪豹，尤其无法回答
这个生命与另一个生命的关系

5

I cannot tell you the name
Of this plant or that animal
Yet I am sure this is a circular world
I know not if the weight on life's scale
Should be nudged a bit to the right
Or nudged a bit to the left
I am just a snow leopard, unable to tell you
The relation of one living thing to another

5

我说不出所有
动物和植物的名字
但这却是一个圆形的世界
我不知道关于生命的天平
应该是，更靠左边一点
还是更靠右边一点，我只是
一只雪豹，尤其无法回答
这个生命与另一个生命的关系

但是我却相信，宇宙的秩序
并非来自偶然和混乱
我与生俱来——
就和羚羊、赤狐、旱獭
有着千丝万缕的依存

But I believe: The order of the cosmos
Does not come from random confusion
Innate with me from birth
Are a thousand threads of reliance
With antelope, red fox and marmot

但是我却相信，宇宙的秩序
并非来自偶然和混乱
我与生俱来——
就和岩羊、赤狐、旱獭
有着千丝万缕的依存

我们不是命运——
在拐弯处的某一个岔路
而更像一个捉摸不透的谜语
我们活在这里已经很长时间
谁也离不开彼此的存在
但是我们却惊恐和惧怕
追逐和新生再没有什么区别……

We are not a bypath where fate turns a corner
We are more like a riddle beyond solving
We have lived here a long time already
Now none can do without the other's existence
Yet we go through startlement and fear
Between the hunt and new life there is no longer a distinction…

我们不是命运——
在拐弯处的某一个岔路
而更像一个捉摸不透的谜语
我们活在这里已经很长时间
谁也离不开彼此的存在
但是我们却惊恐和惧怕
追逐和新生再没有什么区别……

6

我的足迹，留在
雪地上，或许它们的形状
比一串盛开的
梅花还要美丽
或许它是虚无的延伸
因为它，并不指明
其中的奥妙
也不会预言——
未知的结束

6

My tracks left on snowy ground
Have shapes that to some
May have greater beauty
Than a string of plum blossoms
Or they may be extensions of nothingness
Because they point out nothing
About any inherent mystery
And cannot prophesize
A conclusion still unknown

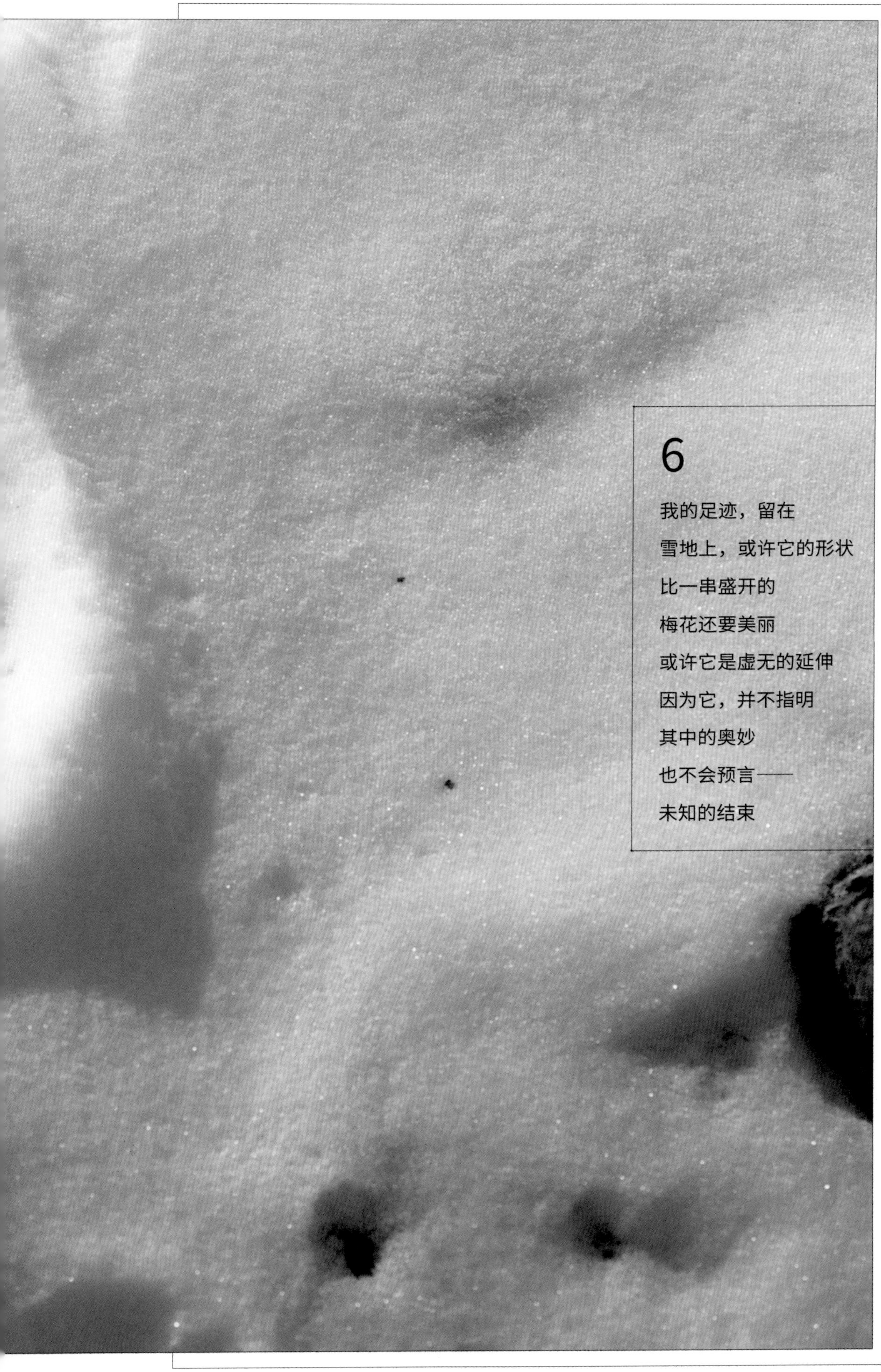

6

我的足迹，留在
雪地上，或许它的形状
比一串盛开的
梅花还要美丽
或许它是虚无的延伸
因为它，并不指明
其中的奥妙
也不会预言——
未知的结束

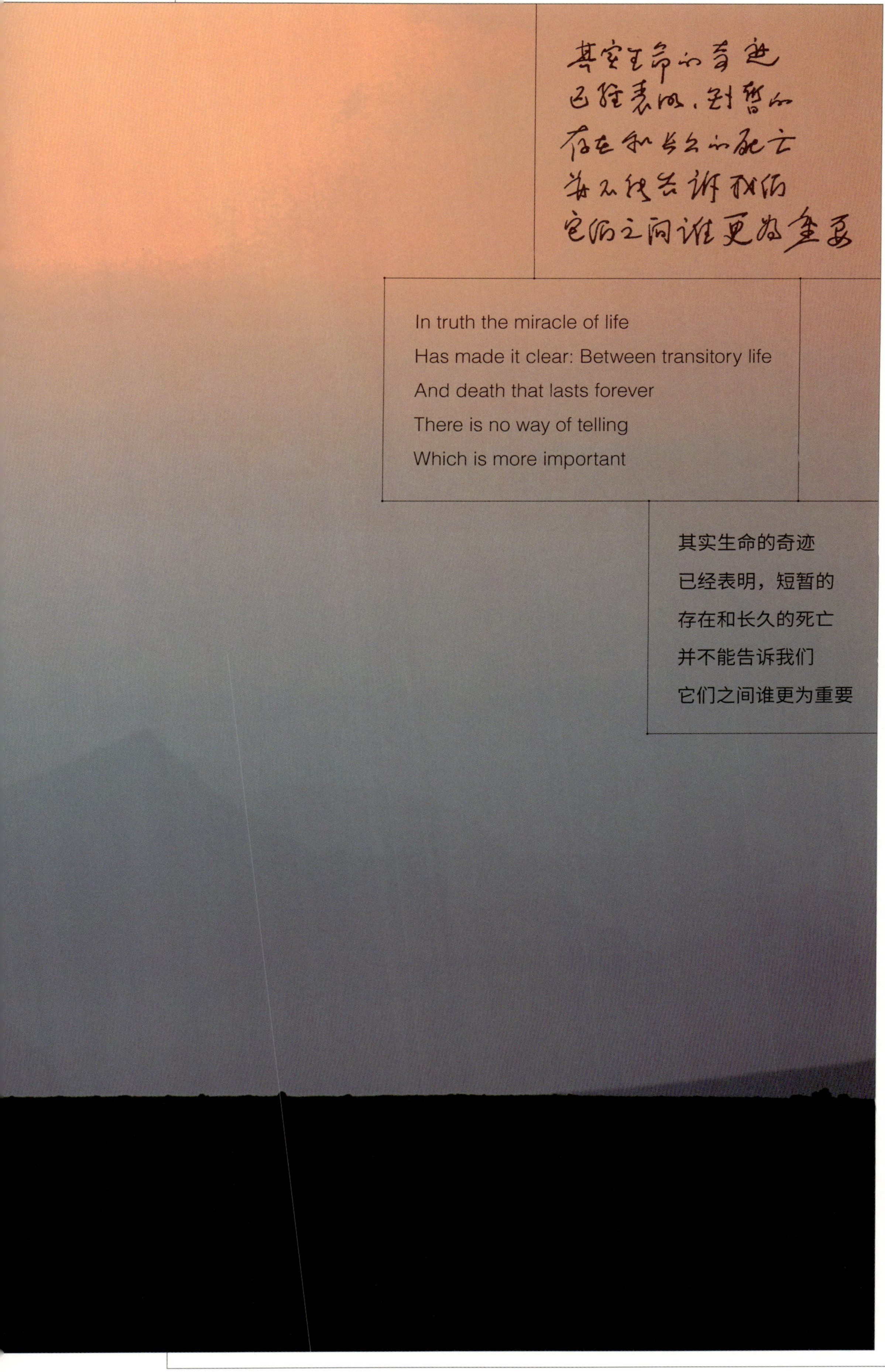

其实生命的奇迹
已经表明，短暂的
存在和长久的死亡
并不能告诉我们
它们之间谁更为重要

In truth the miracle of life
Has made it clear: Between transitory life
And death that lasts forever
There is no way of telling
Which is more important

其实生命的奇迹
已经表明，短暂的
存在和长久的死亡
并不能告诉我们
它们之间谁更为重要

这样的足迹，不是
占卜者留下的，但它是
另一种语言，能发出
寂静的声音

These traces left by paws
Are not marks of a diviner
Yet they are a language, able to pronounce
The voice of silence

这样的足迹，不是
占卜者留下的，但它是
另一种语言，能发出
寂静的声音

唯有起风的时刻，或者
再来一场意想不到的大雪
那些依稀的足迹
才会被一扫而空……

Until a stiff wind bears down
Or a snowstorm steals up
Then this line of fading prints
Will be swept from existence…

唯有起风的时刻，或者
再来一场意想不到的大雪
那些依稀的足迹
才会被一扫而空……

7

当我出现的刹那
你会在死去的记忆中
也许还会在——
刚要苏醒的梦境里
真切而恍惚地看见我：

7

At the instant I appear
I may recur, out of once-dead memory
Or in a dream vision newly wakened
You will glimpse me, genuine yet set apart

7

当我出现的刹那
你会在死去的记忆中
也许还会在——
刚要苏醒的梦境里
真切而恍惚地看见我：

是太阳的反射，光芒的银币
是巨石上的几何，风中的植物
是一朵玫瑰流淌在空气中的颜色
是一千朵玫瑰得以宣泄成的瀑布
是静止的速度，黄金的弧形
I am the sun's reflection, beam from silver coins
Geometry among boulders, a being planted in wind
The color of roses trickling through air
Cataract giving release to a thousand roses
Speed in stillness, golden arc

是太阳的反射，光芒的银币
是岩石上的几何，风中的植物
是一朵玫瑰流淌在空气中的颜色
是一千朵玫瑰最终宣泄成的瀑布
是静止的速度，黄金的弧形

是柔软的时间，碎片的力量
是速度的线条，黑色+白色的可能
是光铸造的画乡，穿越深渊的○
是宇宙失落的长矛，飞行中的箭

Strokeable time, force from brokenness
Incremental contour, black + white made possible
Chieftain stamped in light, "O" that crosses the abyss
Dropped spear of the cosmos, arrow in flight

是柔软的时间，碎片的力量
是过度的线条，黑色+白色的可能
是光铸造的酋长，穿越深渊的O
是宇宙失落的长矛，飞行中的箭

是被感觉和梦幻碰碎的
某一粒逃窜的晶体
水珠四溅，色彩斑斓
是勇士绶带上一颗颗通灵的贝壳
是消失了的国王的头饰
在大地子宫里的又一次复活

A fugitive crystal split away
From wishful dream visions
Flung water-beads, mottled coloring
Telepathic cowries decking a warrior's sash
A king's headpiece gone missing
Again resurrected in the planet's womb

是被感觉和梦幻碰碎的
某一粒逃窜的晶体
水珠四溅，色彩斑斓
是勇士绶带上一颗颗通灵的贝壳
是消失了的国王的头饰
在大地子宫里的又一次复活

8

二月是生命的季节
拒绝羞涩，是燃烧的雪
泛滥的开始
野性的风，吹动峡谷的号角

8

February is the season of life

Says no to shyness

Commences the rampage of burning snow

A wanton wind, blowing its trumpet in a gorge

8

二月是生命的季节

拒绝羞涩，是燃烧的雪

泛滥的开始

野性的风，吹动峡谷的号角

遗忘名字，在这里寻找并完成
另一个生命诞生的仪式
这是所有母性——
神秘的词语和诗篇
它只为生殖之神的
降临而吟诵……

Forgetting names, here seeks and completes
The ceremony for another life to be born
The mysterious psalmody
Of all that is motherly
Coming forth and lifting her voice
Only for the god of fertility...

遗忘名字，在这里寻找并完成
另一个生命诞生的仪式
这是所有母性——
神秘的词语和诗篇
它只为生殖之神的
降临而吟诵……

追逐 离心力 失重 闪电 弧线
欲望的弓 切割的宝石 分裂的空气
重复的跳跃 气味的舌尖 接纳的坚硬
奔跑的目标 颌骨的坡度 不相等的飞行
迟缓的光速 分解的摇曳 缺席的负重
撕咬 撕咬 血管的磷 齿唇的馈赠

Hot pursuit…decentering force…free-fall…lightning flash…arcing
Desire's bow…well-split gem…unresisting air
Exact same leap…tongue tip of scent…hardness for receptivity
Sprint and goal…slope of jaw…unequalled flying
Lingering light-beam…tug of dissolution…burden of absence
Jaws clamping…worrying…phosphor of veins…toothsome gift

追逐 离心力 失重 闪电 弧线
欲望的弓 切割的宝石 分裂的空气
重复的跳跃 气味的舌尖 接纳的坚硬
奔跑的目标 颌骨的坡度 不相等的飞行
迟缓的光速 分解的摇曳 缺席的负重
撕咬 撕咬 血管的磷 齿唇的馈赠

呼啸的波浪 遥远地升起 坚至如初
撞打的舞蹈 悄然死亡的牵引 播放抽空
想象 地震的战栗 奉献 土地的凹陷
向外渗漏 分崩离析 喷泉 喷泉 喷泉
编钟中坠落的传递 边缘的颤抖 回忆
雪鸣后的寂静 等待 群山的回声……

Waves of respiration...abrupt ascent...intensity like the start
Hammering dance...deathly tug at edge...emptying...emptying
Imaginings...earthquake tremors...offering made...concavity of earth
Exfiltration...collapse in pieces...fountain...fountain...fountain...
Weariness of the plunge lived through...edge-walker's tremble...rememorance
Stillness after lightning...waiting...echoes from mountains

呼吸的波浪 急遽地升起 强烈如初
捶打的舞蹈 临界死亡的牵引 抽空 抽空
想象 地震的战栗 奉献 大地的凹陷
向外渗漏 分崩离析 喷泉 喷泉 喷泉
生命中坠落的倦意 边缘的颤抖 回忆
雷鸣后的寂静 等待 群山的回声……

9

在峭壁上奔跑
黑暗的底片
沉落在白昼的海洋
从上到下的逻辑
跳跃虚无与存在的山涧
自由的领地

9

Skipping along a cliff-edge
In the film-negative of darkness
Sinking from sight in daylight's sea
Top to bottom logic of descent
Leaps the ravine of existence and nothingness
Territory of freedom

9

在峭壁上舞蹈

黑暗的底片

沉落在白昼的海洋

从上到下的逻辑

跳跃虚无与存在的山涧

自由的领地

在这里只有我们
能选择自己的方式
我们用四肢攀爬
陡峭的神经
爪子踩着岩石的
琴键，轻如羽毛

Where we are the only ones
To choose our own way
My four limbs clamber
Up the nerve net of a precipice
Paws treading on piano keys
Of boulders, with feather-light moves

在这里只有我们
能选择自己的方式
我的四肢攀爬
陡峭的神经
爪子踩着岩石的
琴键，轻如羽毛

我是山地的幼虫
充满着无尽的渴望
在我生来的时候
风速使石我怯
但我的铠甲却在
空气中嘶嘶发响

I am a sailor of high terrain
Filled with wishes you cannot name
At the moment I strike
The wind's speed cannot rival mine
Yet I have armor all around me
Hear it sighing as air currents blow in

我是山地的水手
充满着无名的渴望
在我出击的时候
风速没有我快
但我的铠甲却在
空气中嘶嘶发响

我是自由落体的王子
雪山十二子的兄弟
九十度地往上冲刺
一百二十度地俯冲下降
是我有着花斑的长尾
平缓了生死的界限……

I am the prince of free-falling objects
Brother among twelve tribes of snow country
Charging upward at 90 degrees
Or in rapid descent at 120 degrees
It is my long, spotted tail that balances me
Just short of death's edge...

The poet is a member of the Nuosu (Yi) ethnicity, and here he refers to a Nuosu text, *The Book of Origins*. In this book's account of creation, earthly life including humans emerged from a snowy region, grouped from the beginning into twelve categories or tribes. (—Tr.)

我是自由落体的王子
雪山十二子的兄弟
九十度地往上冲刺
一百二十度地骤然下降
是我有着花斑的长尾
平衡了生与死的界限……

10

昨晚梦见了妈妈
她还在那里等待，目光幽幽

我们注定是——
孤独的行者

10

Last night I dreamed of Mama
She is still waiting there, that uncanny look in her eyes

We are fated to be
Wayfarers in solitude

10

昨晚梦见了妈妈
她还在那里等待，目光幽幽

我们注定是——
孤独的行者

两岁以后，就会离开保护
独自去证明
我也是一个将比我的父亲
更勇敢的武士
我会为捍卫我高贵血统
以及那世代相传的
永远不可被玷污的荣誉
而流尽最后一滴血

After two years it was time to venture forth
To prove in my own way
I could someday be a warrior
Fighting bigger battles than my father
In defense of my noble bloodline
And of honor that was kept unstained
Down through generations
Let my last drop of blood be shed

两岁以后，就会离开保护
独自去证明
我也是一个将比我的父亲
更勇敢的武士
我会为捍卫我高贵血统
以及那世代相传的
永远不可被玷污的荣誉
而流尽最后一滴血

我们不会选择耻辱
就是在决斗的沙场
我也会在临死前
大声地告诉世人
——我是谁的儿子！

I will never choose a path of shame
At the fatal scene of all-out battle
Before I meet my death
I will loudly tell the world
Whose son I am!

我们不会选择耻辱
就是在决斗的沙场
我也会在临死前
大声地告诉世人
——我是谁的儿子！

因为祖先的英名
如同白雪一样圣洁
从出生的那一天
我就明白——
我和我的兄弟们
是一座座雪山
永远的保护神

And that my forefathers' heroic names
Have the holy purity of snow
From the day of my birth
I already understood
That my brothers and I
Would forever be guardian deities
Of each snow peak

因为祖先的英名
如同白雪一样圣洁
从出生的那一天
我就明白——
我和我的兄弟们
是一座座雪山
永远的保护神

我们不会遗忘——
神圣的职责
我们梦境里时常浮现的
是一代代祖先的容貌
我们双肩上担当着的
是一个伟大家族的
黄金谱系！

我总是靠近死亡，但也凝视未来

I will never forget
This sacred calling
In dreams floating before me
A chain of faces stretches far back
And from between my lips
Reverberates the golden genealogy
Of a grand family line

我们不会遗忘——
神圣的职责
我的梦境里时常浮现的
是一代代祖先的容貌
我的双唇上飘荡着的
是一个伟大家族的
黄金谱系！

I always verge upon death, yet keep eyes on the future

我总是靠近死亡，但也凝视未来

11

有人说我护卫的神山
没有雪灾和瘟疫
当我独自站在山巅
在目光所及之地
白雪一片清澈

11

Some say the mountain god I serve
Inflicts no plagues or snow disasters
Standing by myself on a peak
Whichever way I turn
My eyes are met by pristine snow

11

有人说我护卫的神山
没有雪灾和瘟疫
当我独自站在山巅
在目光所及之地
白雪一片清澈

所有的生命都沐浴在纯净的
祥和的光里。远方的鹰
最初还能看见，在无际的边缘
只剩下一个小点，但是，还是同往常一样
在蓝色的深处，消失得无影无踪

All creatures are bathed in pure, benign light
And a distant eagle dwindles
A watcher whose eyes follow that dot
At some point loses track in blue depths

所有的生命都沐浴在纯净的
祥和的光里。远方的鹰
最初还能看见，在无际的边缘
只剩下一个小点，但是，还是同往常一样
在蓝色的深处，消失得无影无踪

在不远的地方，牧人的炊烟
袅袅推升，几乎看不出这是一种现实
黑色的牦牛，散落在山凹的低洼中
在那里，会有一些紫色的雾霭，飘浮
在小河白色冰层的上面

Not too far below, cooking smoke of herdsmen
Wafts upward, hardly suggesting the workaday world
Black yaks are peppered about in boggy hollows
Down there a bluish haze floats
Over rime-ice of a small river

在不远的地方，牧人的炊烟
袅袅轻升，几乎看不出这是一种现实
黑色的牦牛，散落在山凹的低洼中
在那里，会有一些紫色的雾霭，飘浮
在小河白色冰层的上面

在这样的时候，灵魂和肉体已经分离
我的思绪，开始忘我地漂浮
此时，仿佛能听到来自天宇的声音
而我的舌尖上的词语，正用另一种方式
在这苍穹巨大的穹幕，开始
为这一片大地上的所有生灵祈祷……

At such times, spirit and flesh go their own ways
I am absorbed in my unwinding thought-trains
Now sounds from the firmament seem audible
Here at this giant portal leading to the sky-vault
Words on my tongue tip, after their own fashion
Begin praying for all creatures on this land

在这样的时候，灵魂和肉体已经分离
我的思绪，开始忘我地漂浮
此时，仿佛能听到来自天宇的声音
而我的舌尖上的词语，正用另一种方式
在这苍穹巨大的门前，开始
为这一片大地上的所有生灵祈福……

12

我活在典籍里，是岩石中的蛇
我的命是一百匹马的命，是一千头牛的命
也是一万个人的命。因为我，隐蔽在
佛经的某一页，谁杀死我，就是
杀死另一个看不见的，成千上万的我
我的血迹不会留在巨石上，因为它
没有颜色，但那样仍然是罪证

12

I also live in classic texts, called “snake among crags”
My life is worth a hundred horses, a thousand cows
Even ten thousand humans, for a verse
Hidden in a scripture says, whoever kills me
Kills an unseen me that takes a thousand forms
This self will not leave blood on boulders
For it has no color, yet to kill it would be sinful

12

我活在典籍里，是岩石中的蛇
我的命是一百匹马的命，是一千头牛的命
也是一万个人的命。因为我，隐蔽在
佛经的某一页，谁杀死我，就是
杀死另一个看不见的，成千上万的我
我的血迹不会留在巨石上，因为它
没有颜色，但那样仍然是罪证

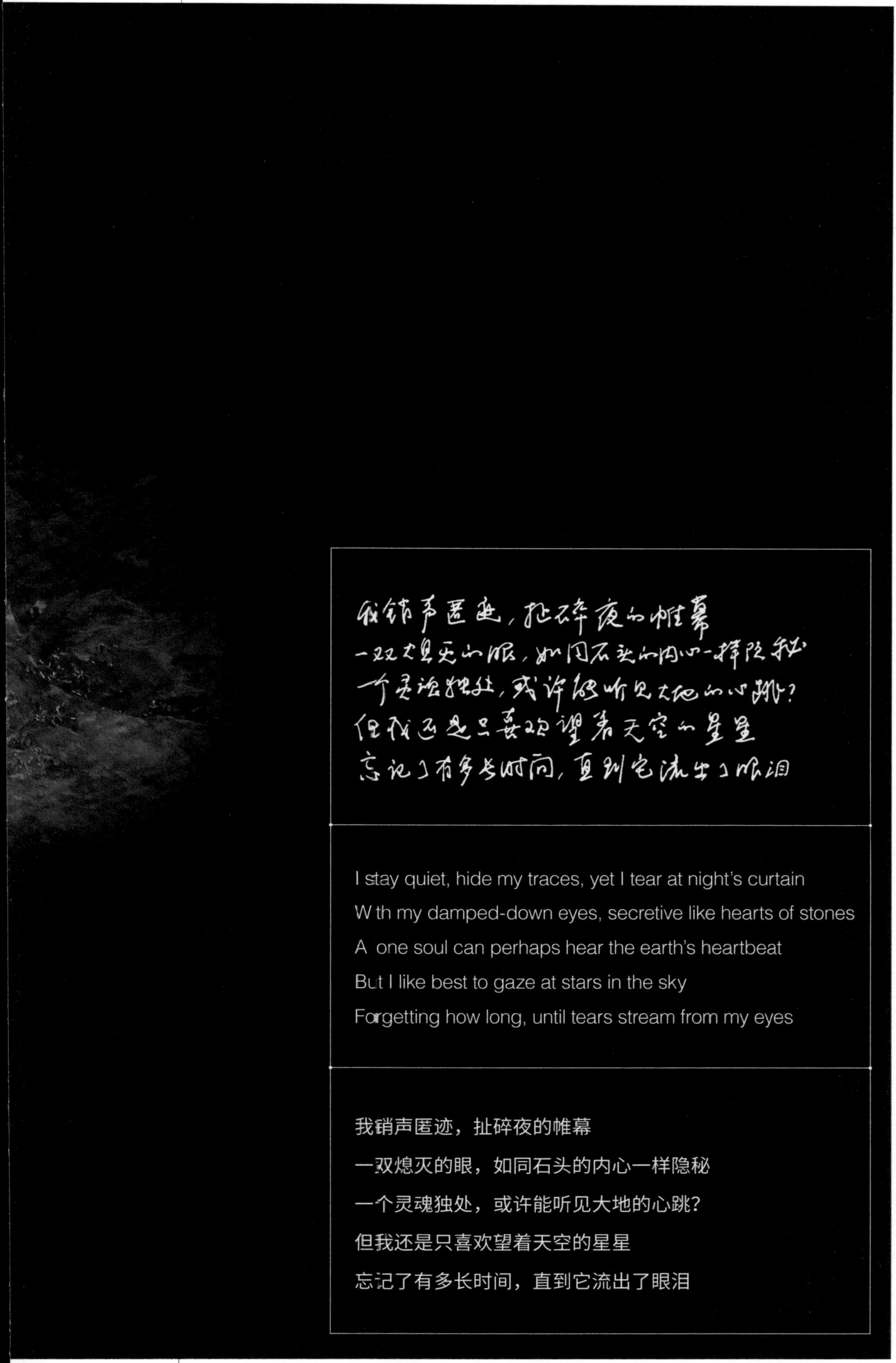

I stay quiet, hide my traces, yet I tear at night's curtain
With my damped-down eyes, secretive like hearts of stones
Alone soul can perhaps hear the earth's heartbeat
But I like best to gaze at stars in the sky
Forgetting how long, until tears stream from my eyes

我销声匿迹，扯碎夜的帷幕
一双熄灭的眼，如同石头的内心一样隐秘
一个灵魂独处，或许能听见大地的心跳？
但我还是只喜欢望着天空的星星
忘记了有多长时间，直到它流出了眼泪

13

一颗子弹击中了
我的兄弟，那只名字叫白银的雪豹
射击者的手指，弯曲着
一陣沉闷的牛角的回声
已把死亡的讯息传遍了山谷

13

A deadly bullet was fired
At my brother, the snow leopard named White Silver
The gunman just crooked his finger
And echoes of a grim trumpet
Spread news of death through the valley

13

一颗子弹击中了
我的兄弟，那只名字叫白银的雪豹
射击者的手指，弯曲着
一阵沉闷的牛角的回声
已把死亡的讯息传遍了山谷

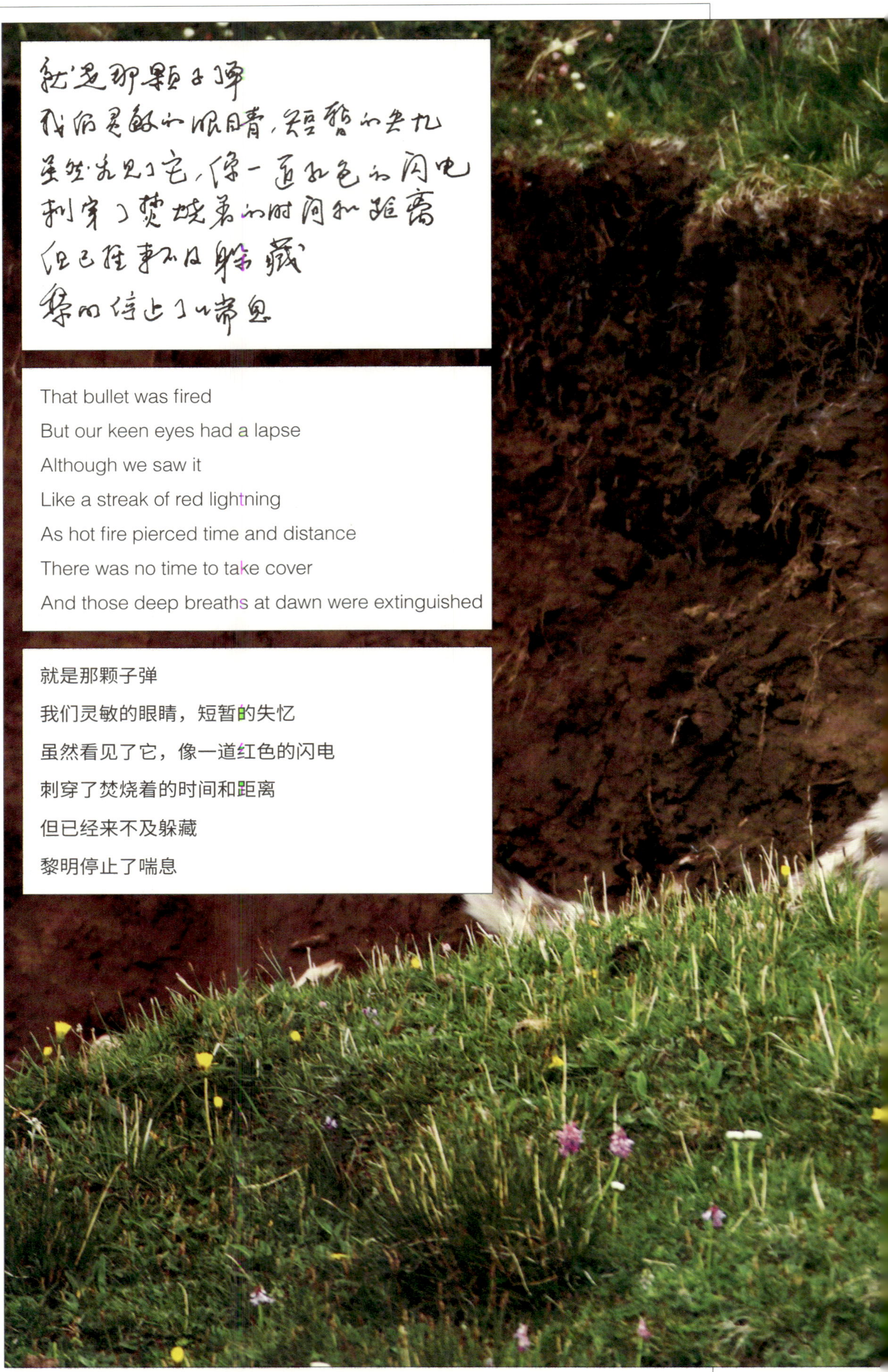

就是那颗子弹
我们灵敏的眼睛，短暂的失忆
虽然看见了它，像一道红色的闪电
刺穿了焚烧着的时间和距离
但已经来不及躲藏
黎明停止了喘息

That bullet was fired
But our keen eyes had a lapse
Although we saw it
Like a streak of red lightning
As hot fire pierced time and distance
There was no time to take cover
And those deep breaths at dawn were extinguished

就是那颗子弹
我们灵敏的眼睛，短暂的失忆
虽然看见了它，像一道红色的闪电
刺穿了焚烧着的时间和距离
但已经来不及躲藏
黎明停止了喘息

就是那颗子弹
它的发射来的头颅，以及
为这个头颅供给血液的心脏
已经被罪恶的眼睛冻结

The bullet was fired, and so
The gunman's skull and the heart
That supplied his skull with blood
Are now frozen forever within annals of sin

就是那颗子弹
它的发射者的头颅，以及
为这个头颅供给血液的心脏
已经被罪恶的账簿冻结

就是那颗子弹，像一滴血
就在它穿透目标的那一个瞬间
射杀者也将被眼前的景象震撼
在子弹飞过的地方
群山的哭泣发出伤口的声音
赤狐的悲鸣再没有停止
岩石上流淌着晶莹的泪水
蒿草吹响了死亡的笛子
冰河在不该碎裂的时候开始巨响
天空出现了地狱的颜色
恐惧的雷声滚动在黑暗的天际

Because of that bloody bullet
At the instant it pierced its target
The gunman would be shaken by the sight
And where the bullet flew
Sobbing mountains would sound like a wound
The red fox's keening continues up to now
Crystalline teardrops trickle on boulders
Wormwood blows the flute-song of death
A buckling glacier booms out of season
Colors of hell appear in the sky
Thunder of dread rolls at the dark skyline

就是那颗子弹，像一滴血
就在它穿透目标的那一个瞬间
射杀者也将被眼前的景象震撼
在子弹飞过的地方
群山的哭泣发出伤口的声音
赤狐的悲鸣再没有停止
岩石上流淌着晶莹的泪水
蒿草吹响了死亡的笛子
冰河在不该碎裂的时候开始巨响
天空出现了地狱的颜色
恐惧的雷声滚动在黑暗的天际

我们的每一次死亡，都是生命的控诉！

With each of our deaths, life brings an indictment!

我们的每一次死亡，都是生命的控诉！

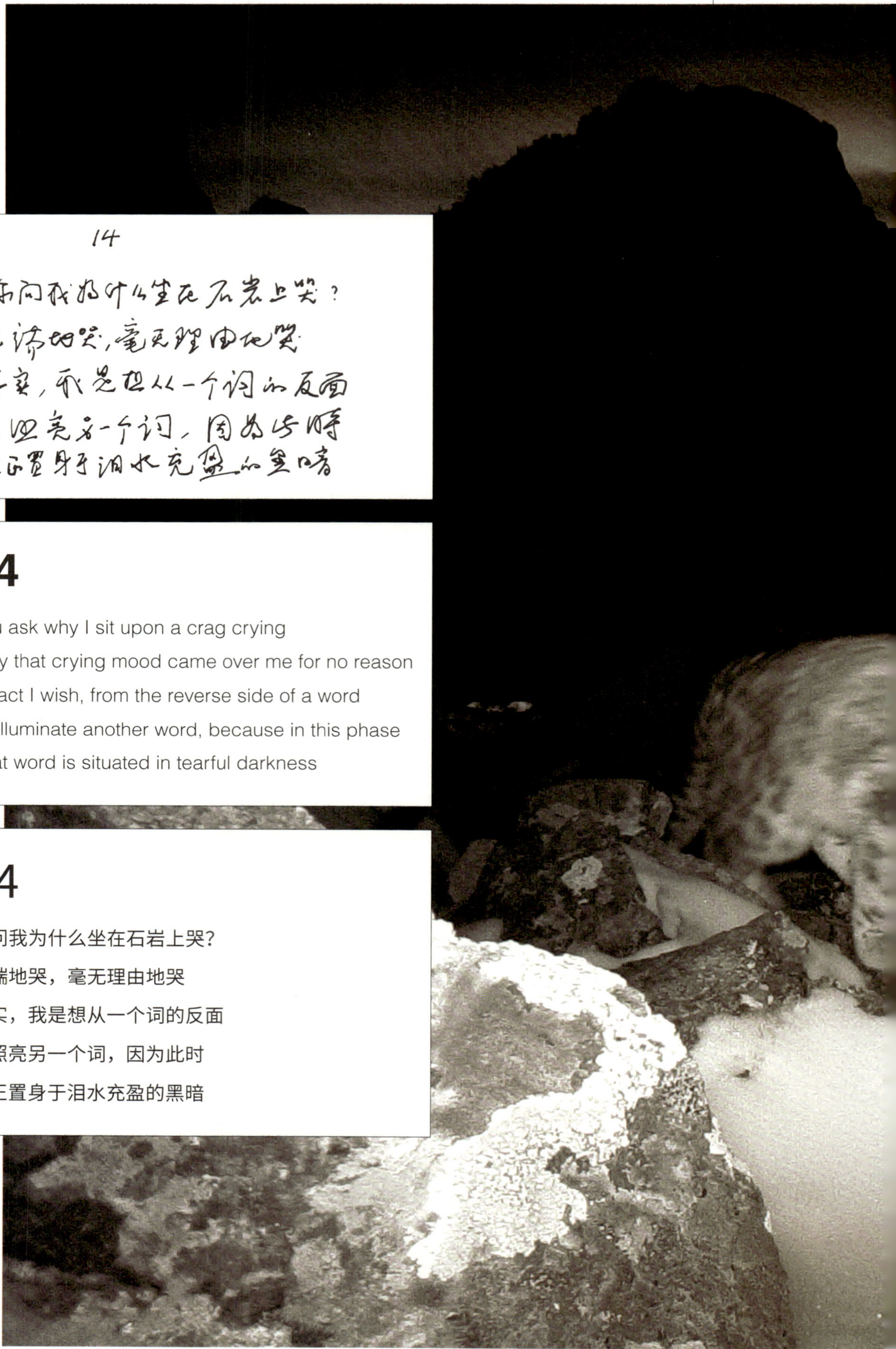

14

你问我为什么坐在石岩上哭？
无端地哭，毫无理由地哭
其实，我是想从一个词的反面
去照亮另一个词，因为此时
它正置身于泪水充盈的黑暗

14

You ask why I sit upon a crag crying
Why that crying mood came over me for no reason
In fact I wish, from the reverse side of a word
To illuminate another word, because in this phase
That word is situated in tearful darkness

14

你问我为什么坐在石岩上哭?
无端地哭，毫无理由地哭
其实，我是想从一个词的反面
去照亮另一个词，因为此时
它正置身于泪水充盈的黑暗

我要把埋在石岩阴影里的头
从雾的深处抬起，用一双敏感的眼睛
机警地审视危机四伏的世界
所有生存的方式，都来自祖先的传承
在这里古老的太阳，给了我们温暖
伸手就能触摸的，是低垂的月亮
同样是它们，用一种宽厚的仁慈
让我们学会了万物的语言，通灵的技艺

This head of mine, buried in shadows of boulders—
Let me raise it out of fog, and with questioning eyes
Scrutinize the lurking dangers of our world
Our ways of surviving came down from our forefathers
The immemorial sun provides us with warmth
Within closer reach are those low-hanging moons
They too show kindness through the seasons and help us
To heed the language of all things, to commune with spirits

我要把埋在石岩阴影里的头
从雾的深处抬起，用一双疑惑的眼睛
机警地审视危机四伏的世界
所有生存的方式，都来自祖先的传承
在这里古老的太阳，给了我们温暖
伸手就能触摸的，是低垂的月亮
同样是它们，用一种宽厚的仁慈
让我们学会了万物的语言，通灵的技艺

是的，我们渐渐地已经知道
这个世界亘古就有的自然法则
开始被人类一天天地改变
钢铁的声音，以及摩天大楼的倒影
在这个地球绿色的肺叶上
留下了血淋淋的伤口，我们还能看见
就在每一分钟的时空里
都有着动物和植物的灭绝在发生

Indeed it has come to our knowledge
That nature's timeless laws over this world
Are being altered every day by mankind
Clang of steel and shadow of high rises
On the green lungs of this planet
Have left bloody wounds, and we can see
With every passing year
Extinction of creatures is happening

是的，我们渐渐地已经知道
这个世界亘古就有的自然法则
开始被人类一天天地改变
钢铁的声音，以及摩天大楼的倒影
在这个地球绿色的肺叶上
留下了血淋淋的伤口，我们还能看见
就在每一分钟的时空里
都有着动物和植物的灭绝在发生

我们知道，时间已经不多
无论是对于人类，还是对于我们自己
或许这已经就是最后的机会
因为这个地球全部生命的延续，已经证实
任何一种动物和植物的消亡
都是我们共同的灾难和梦魇
在这里，我想告诉人类
我们大家都已无路可逃，这也是
你看见我只身坐在岩石上，为什么
失声痛哭的原因！

We know there is not much time left
Not for humankind, not for ourselves
Maybe this is already our last chance
Because the course of all life on earth attests
To let any kind of plant or animal fade away
Would threaten disaster for all in common
Here is what I would wish to tell human beings
There is no escape route for any of us
This is why you see me here alone
Sitting on a crag, racked by sobs!

我们知道，时间已经不多
无论是对于人类，还是对于我们自己
或许这已经就是最后的机会
因为这个地球全部生命的延续，已经证实
任何一种动物和植物的消亡
都是我们共同的灾难和梦魇
在这里，我想告诉人类
我们大家都已无路可逃，这也是
你看见我只身坐在岩石上，为什么
失声痛哭的原因！

15

我是另一种存在，常常看不见自己
除了在灰色的岩石上重返
最喜爱的还是，繁星点点的夜空
因为这无限的天际
像我美丽的身躯，幻化成的图案

15

I am a curious kind of being, often unable to see myself
Unless I get back among these dun-colored crags
Most of all I like the night sky thick with stars
Because the sky's boundless reaches
Lock like this lovely coat, these designs spun from the void

15

我是另一种存在，常常看不见自己
除了在灰色的岩石上重返
最喜爱的还是，繁星点点的夜空
因为这无限的天际
像我美丽的身躯，幻化成的图案

为了证实自己的发现
轻轻地呼吸，我会从一千里之外
闻到草原花草的香甜
迅速在瞬间，分辨出羚羊消失的方位
甚至有时候，能够准确预测
是谁的蹄印，落在了山涧的底部

To confirm my own discovery
I sniff the air and catch a scent
Of sweet grassland flowers hundreds of miles away
In a wink I can detect where an antelope took cover
At times I can accurately foresee
Whose hoof will alight at the bottom of that ravine

为了证实自己的发现
轻轻地呼吸，我会从一千里之外
闻到草原花草的香甜
还能在瞬间，分辨出羚羊消失的方位
甚至有时候，能够准确预测
是谁的蹄印，落在了山涧的底部

我能听见微尘的声音
在它的核心，有巨石碎裂
还有若隐若现的银河
永不复返地熄灭
那千万个深不见底的黑洞
闪耀着未知的白昼

I can hear the sound of a dust mote
At its core was a giant rock that split
And further in a galaxy, barely an inkling
Now irrevocably extinguished
And the bottomless depths of countless black holes
Holding muted refulgence of yet unknown daybreaks

我能听见微尘的声音
在它的核心，有巨石碎裂
还有若隐若现的银河
永不复返地熄灭
那千万个深不见底的黑洞
闪耀着未知的白昼

我能在睡梦中，进入濒临死亡的状态
那时候能看见，转世前的模样
为了减轻沉重的罪孽，我也曾经
把赎罪的钟声敲响

虽然我有九条命，但死亡的来临
也将同来世的新生一样正常……

In dreamy sleep, I enter a near-death state
There I see my pre-incarnated form
To lighten the heavy load of sin, I too
Once rang the bells of redemption

Despite my nine lives, the coming of my death
Will be a matter of course, just like my next birth...

我能在睡梦中，进入濒临死亡的状态
那时候能看见，转世前的模样
为了减轻沉重的罪孽，我也曾经
把赎罪的钟声敲响

虽然我有九条命，但死亡的来临
也将同来世的新生一样正常……

16

我不会写文字的诗
但我们也会——用自己的脚趾
在这白雪皑皑的素笺上
为未来的子孙，留下
自己最后的遗言

16

I cannot compose poems in writing
Yet I am able—using my own paws
On unruled stationery of glittery snow
To leave my last will and testament
For sons and grandsons to come

16

我不会写文字的诗
但我仍然会——用自己的脚趾
在这白雪皑皑的素笺上
为未来的子孙，留下
自己最后的遗言

我的一生，就如同我们所有的
先辈和前贤一样，熟悉并了解
雪域世界的一切，在这里
黎明的曙光，要远远比黄昏的落日
还要诱人，那完全是
因为白雪反光的作用
不是在每一个季节，我们都能
享受幸福的时光
或许，这就是命运和生活的无常
有时还会为获取生存的食物
被尖利的碎石划伤
但尽管如此，我欢乐的日子
还是要比悲伤的时日更多

Like my admired forefathers
It has taken me a lifetime to learn
All I need to understand of this snowy region
Here the glow of coming dawn
Due to reflectivity of snow
Is more enticing than dusky sunset
Blessed times may not be ours to enjoy
In every month of every season
Such is the impermanence of life and fate
Sometimes to catch food for survival
We receive cuts from sharp-edged stones
Even so our joyful days
Outnumber our days of sorrow

我的一生，就如同我们所有的
先辈和前贤一样，熟悉并了解
雪域世界的一切，在这里
黎明的曙光，要远远比黄昏的落日
还要诱人，那完全是
因为白雪反光的作用
不是在每一个季节，我们都能
享受幸福的时光
或许，这就是命运和生活的无常
有时还会为获取生存的食物
被尖利的碎石划伤
但尽管如此，我欢乐的日子
还是要比悲伤的时日更多

我曾去见过许多壮丽的景象
可以说，是这个世界别的动物
当然也包括人类，闻所未闻
不是因为我的欲望所获
而是伟大的造物主对我的厚爱
在这雪山的最高处，我曾见过
凝固的时间，在盈雪的光辉里消失
如此灿烂的星群，像浮出芬芳的甘露
有一束光，那来自宇宙的纤维
是如何渐渐地融入了永恒的黑暗

I have seen so many grand views
It is safe to say, no other animal in the world
Not even humans of course, could conceive of them
Such views were not gained by my own desire
But through generosity of the great creator
On the heights of these snowy mountains I have seen
Time in a liquid state, gathered into blue-tinged snowpack
Splendid star-fields that emanate bracing scents of dew
And how light beams, starting from the very fibers of the cosmos
Will eventually fall into eternal darkness

我曾看见过许多壮丽的景象
可以说，是这个世界别的动物
当然也包括人类，闻所未闻
不是因为我的欲望所获
而是伟大的造物主对我的厚爱
在这雪山的最高处，我看见过
液态的时间，在蓝雪的光辉里消失
灿烂的星群，倾泻出芬芳的甘露
有一束光，那来自宇宙的纤维
是如何渐渐地落入了永恒的黑暗

是的，我还要告诉你一个秘密
我没有看见过地狱完整的模样
但我却找到了通往天堂的入口！

Indeed, I am here to tell you my secret
I have not seen Hell in any coherent shape
But I found an entranceway leading to Heaven!

是的，我还要告诉你一个秘密
我没有看见过地狱完整的模样
但我却找到了通往天堂的入口！

17

这不是告别
原谅我！我永远不会离开这里
尽管这是最后的领地
我偏离群索居，在人迹罕至的地方

17

This is not a farewell

Bear with me! Never will I leave this final territory

Though I have been pushed back many times

I will go off and live alone, where human traces seldom come

17

这不是道别

原谅我！我永远不会离开这里

尽管这是最后的领地

我将离群索居，在人迹罕至的地方

Do not hunt me down
Here on this planetary world, for I am your brother
Connected to you by blood and bone
Before dark wings come to envelop me
Let me forget the terror of slaughter

不要再追杀我，我也是这个
星球世界，与你们的骨血
连在一起的同胞兄弟
让我在黑色的翅膀笼罩之前
忘记虐杀带来的恐惧

当我们从祖先千年的记忆中醒来
神授的语言，滑过我们双唇
变成道具，那父子连名的传统
在今天，已成为反对一切强权的武器

In my forefathers' long fund of memory, as I myself awake
Spirit-given language makes my lips into ritual vessels
And my name linked to my father's name
Now becomes a weapon against naked power!

当我从祖先千年的记忆中醒来
神授的语言，将把我的双唇
变成道具，那父子连名的传统
在今天，已成为反对一切强权的武器

原谅我！我不需要廉价的同情
我的历史、价值体系以及独特的生活方式
是我在这个大千世界里
立足的根本所在，谁也不能代替！

Bear with me! I need no facile sympathy
My history and way of life, by my own values,
Is what I stand by
In this world of worlds, brooking no substitute!

原谅我！我不需要廉价的同情
我的历史、价值体系以及独特的生活方式
是我在这个大千世界里
立足的根本所在，谁也不能代替！

不要把我的图片放在
众人都能看见的地方
我害怕，那些以保护的名义
对我进行的看不见的追逐和同化！

Do not display my picture
In places where the crowd can see it
I fear their covert pursuit and claims on me
All done in the name of protection

不要把我的图片放在
众人都能看见的地方
我害怕，那些以保护的名义
对我进行的看不见的追逐和同化！

原谅我！这不是道别
但是我相信，那最后的审判
绝不会遥遥无期……！

2014年2月14日—18日于昆明
匆匆草就。重抄于2018年
11月25日—26日北京。

Bear with me! This is not a farewell
But I believe: The time until final judgment
Will not be dragged out endlessly…!

February 14-18, 2014
Written in haste, Kunming.
Recopied in Beijing,
November 25—26, 2018.

原谅我！这不是道别
但是我相信，那最后的审判
绝不会遥遥无期……！

2014年2月14日—18日
于昆明匆匆草就。
重抄于2018年11月25日—26日北京。

关于雪豹

雪豹(*Panthera uncia*)英文名 snow leopard，因其常在高原雪线附近和雪地间活动而得名。雪豹行动敏捷，善于攀岩，昼伏夜出，行踪隐秘，被称为“雪山之王”“雪山上的精灵”。

雪豹属于脊索动物门，哺乳动物纲，食肉目，猫科，雪豹属。国家一级保护动物。

雪豹是亚洲高山地区的特有物种，是全世界分布海拔最高的大型猫科动物，是高山生态系统的关键种、旗舰种和伞护种。

雪豹为斑状分布，分布于亚洲的12个国家和地区，包括中国、哈萨克斯坦、乌兹别克斯坦、塔吉克斯坦、吉尔吉斯斯坦、蒙古、阿富汗、印度、尼泊尔、巴基斯坦等地，历史上在缅甸曾有分布。

据世界自然保护联盟(IUCN)推算，中国的雪豹种群可能在2 000~2 500只。中国雪豹种群数量和栖息地面积均占全球50%以上。

中国雪豹分布于西藏、四川、新疆、青海、甘肃、宁夏、内蒙古、云南等省区的高海拔地区，如喜马拉雅山、冈底斯山、天山、帕米尔高原、昆仑山、唐古拉山、阿尔泰山、阿尔金山、祁连山、贺兰山、阴山等。在平原地区偶尔也有其踪迹。

雪豹是典型的独居动物，具有较强的领地意识，但相邻个体的领地常出现部分重叠。每年1月—3月为雪豹发情期。受孕后，它们一般每年5月—6月产崽，每胎1～3崽，2～3年性成熟，寿命在10年左右。一般情况下，成年雪豹仅在发情期成对活动。

雪豹处于高原山地生态系统食物链的顶端，主要捕食岩羊、盘羊、北山羊、白唇鹿、马麝等偶蹄类食草动物，也捕食旱獭、高原兔、鼠兔、雉类及其他啮齿类动物。冬末春初等食物匮乏的季节，它们也偷袭家畜。与雪豹一起生活在高原山地的食肉动物和猛禽，包括狼、棕熊、赤狐、猞猁、草原雕、玉带海雕、胡兀鹫等，它们会与雪豹竞争捕食猎物，或抢夺、偷取雪豹捕杀后的猎物与残骸。

与雪豹同域分布的动物多属于高山草甸草原、寒漠动物群，它们大多能适应与雪豹天然栖息地类似的环境，因而保持了较高的种群数量。这里的动物常有相似的习性，如穴居、冬眠、储草和迁徙等。

雪豹作为生态区位的顶级捕食者，通过捕猎老弱病残的猎物来有效控制和调节野生有蹄类动物的种群数量，对维护高原生态系统的平衡和健康稳定发挥着十分重要的作用。

雪豹所分布的中国西部高海拔地区，包含丰富独特的生物多样性，保护雪豹这一高山生态系统的关键物种，有助于保护包括中国人口在内的亚洲数十亿人口的饮水安全和生态安全。

为加强对雪豹及其生态系统的保护，中国不仅颁布了一系列的保护法律法规，而且实施了严格的执法监察，并组织开展针对雪豹的科研监测，严厉打击盗猎走私。已建成各级雪豹自然保护区30余处，并正在开展祁连山国家公园体制试点工作，对雪豹等濒危野生动物种群及其生态系统实施全面、完整、连续的保护，探索保护新途径。中国还与各雪豹分布国共同推动落实“全球雪豹及其生态系统保护计划”，开展了大量卓有成效的工作，使得雪豹及其栖息地保护现出曙光。

雪豹，人类的朋友。我们会好好爱你的。

About the snow leopard

The snow leopard *(Panthera uncia)* is named as it inhabits the alpine and subalpine zones of high mountains where there is snow covering. It is agile, good at rock climbing, nocturnal and elusive – thus given the nicknames as "the king of snow mountain" "the mountain ghost".

The snow leopard is classified as follows: Phylum: Chordata; Class: Mammalia; Order: Carnivora; Family: Felidae; and Genus: Panthera. In China, it is listed as a Class I protected species of the national government.

The snow leopard is a unique species only found in the high mountains of Asia. It is a big cat living in the highest altitude. It is the keystone species, flagship species and umbrella species of alpine montane ecosystems.

Snow leopards have a patchy distribution throughout twelve countries and districts in Asia, i.e. China, Kazakhstan, Uzbekistan, Tajikistan, Kyrgyzstan, Mongolia, Afghanistan, India, Nepal, Pakistan, etc. Historically, they were also found in Myanmar.

According to the International Union for Conservation of Nature (IUCN), China's snow leopard population is estimated at 2,000 to 2,500 individuals. China's snow leopard population and habitat area both account for more than 50% of the world's snow leopard population and habitat area.

In China, they are distributed in the mountain ranges of Tibet, Sichuan, Xinjiang, Qinghai, Gansu, Ningxia, Inner Mongolia and Yunnan provinces, such as the Himalayas, Gangdise Shan, Tian Shan, Pamirs, Kunlun Mountains, Tanggula Mountains, Altai Mountains, Altun Mountains, Qilian Mountains, Helan Mountains, Yin Mountains, etc. There are occasional traces in the plains.

Snow leopards are typical solitary animals and can be quite territorial. However, territories of neighbouring individuals often overlap partially. The oestrous cycle for snow leopards occurs between January and March annually. If conceived, females would give birth to the cubs between May and June. Litter sizes vary from one to three. They become sexually mature at two to three years, and the life expectancy is generally about ten years. In most cases, adult snow leopards only live in pairs when in oestrus.

The snow leopard is a top predator of the alpine montane ecosystem. It preys mainly on even-toed ungulates, such as bharal, argali, Siberian ibex, Thorold's deer and Alpine musk deer. It also hunts marmot, woolly hare, pika, phasianids and other rodents. During late winter or when their wild prey is scarce, snow leopards will prey on domestic livestock. They face challenges from other carnivores and raptors, including wolves, brown bear, red fox, Eurasian lynx, steppe eagle, Pallas's fish eagle and bearded-vulture, as they compete with snow leopards for prey. They also rob or steal the snow leopard's kill.

Most of the animals that inhabit the same range as snow leopards belong to the alpine meadows and mountain tundra fauna, which makes them adaptable to the environment similar to the natural habitat of snow leopards, thus maintaining a high population. These animals often have similar habits, such as burrowing, hibernation and migration.

As an apex predator, the snow leopard effectively controls and regulates the ungulate population number by predating on old, weak or sick individuals. This plays an important role in maintaining the balance and stability of the high-mountain ecosystems.

In the alpine region of western China where snow leopards inhabit, there is also a rich and indigenous biodiversity. By protecting the keystone species of this region, i.e. the snow leopard, it helps to safeguard the ecological security, as well as water security of billions of Asians including China.

China has taken several measures to reinforce the protection of snow leopards and their ecosystems. This includes enactment of a series of protection laws and regulations, strict law enforcement and supervision, and scientific research and monitoring on snow leopards. There is also been a series of crackdowns on poaching and smugglings. More than thirty snow leopard nature reserves have been designated, and pilot program of Qilian Mountain National Park was launched to implement comprehensive and continuous protection on endangered wildlife, such as snow leopards, and their ecosystems. This program also seeks to explore new ways of protection. Moreover, China is working together with other snow leopard range countries to promote the implementation of the "Global Snow Leopard and Ecosystem Protection Program". Lots of constructive works have been implemented as a result of the joint initiative, making the future of the snow leopard more promising.

Snow leopards, the friends of human, should be loved.

图录引言

本书图片由“自然影像中国”提供。

“自然影像中国”是由中国野生动物保护协会、飞羽视界、中国(林业)生态摄影协会发起的一个面向大众的自然保护与传播项目。其主旨是用影像展现中国丰富美丽的野生动植物和自然生态奇观，尤其是中国特有珍稀的物种。

这些图片有的出自国内外著名自然生态摄影师之手，有的是一线林业工作人员、护林员的巡护记录，还有的是科研和动物保护组织的研究工作成果，许多图片为首次公开。

雪豹大多生活在荒无人烟的雪域高原，数量稀少，加之雪豹生性敏感，皮毛花色易于隐入周边环境，因此拍摄雪豹极具挑战性。许多拍摄者在海拔4 000米以上的高原爬冰卧雪，风餐露宿，历经艰险，寻觅守候数十天甚至数月，才能为读者奉献这些难得一见的精彩照片。

在此，我们对为本书提供图片的拍摄者表示衷心的感谢，并向他们致以崇高的敬意！

The photos in this book are provided by Natural Image China.

Natural Image China is a nature conservation and communication project initiated by the China Wildlife Conservation Association, Feiyu Visions and China (Forestry) Eco-Photography Association. Its main purpose is to use images to showcase China's rich wildlife and stunning natural wonders, especially the rare and unique species of China.

Some of these photos were taken by well-known international nature photographers as well as Chinese nature photographers, while some were the first-hand records of forest workers and rangers. There is also research work came from scientific studies and wildlife protection organizations. Many of them are published for the first time.

Due to their elusive and shy nature, and their scarce number in the remote mountains, the photograph shooting of snow leopards can be very challenging. Many photographers often have to search for days, or even months, under freezing temperatures before they could take a shot of the elusive creature.

Here, we would like to express our heartfelt thanks to the photographers who provided these wonderful photos and honour them for their hard work.

自然影像中国
Nature Image China

雪豹
Snow leopard (*Panthera uncia*)
谢建国　摄
Photo by Xie Jianguo
青海
Qinghai

雪豹
Snow leopard (*Panthera uncia*)
杰德·威恩嘉顿　摄
Photo by Jed Weingarten
四川
Sichuan

天山山脉
Tianshan Mountains
桑布　摄
Photo by Sang Bu
新疆
Xinjiang

雪豹
Snow leopard (*Panthera uncia*)
杰德·威恩嘉顿　摄
Photo by Jed Weingarten
青海
Qinghai

雪豹
Snow leopard (*Panthera uncia*)
谢建国　摄
Photo by Xie Jianguo
青海
Qinghai

唐古拉山脉
Tanggula Mountains
谢建国　摄
Photo by Xie Jianguo
青海
Qinghai

昆仑山河谷
Broad valley in Kunlun Mountains
杰德·威恩嘉顿　摄
Photo by Jed Weingarten
青海
Qinghai

金雕
Golden eagle (*Aquila chrysaetos*)
谢建国　摄
Photo by Xie Jianguo
青海
Qinghai

唐古拉山脉
Tanggula Mountains
谢建国　摄
Photo by Xie Jianguo
青海
Qinghai

雪豹
Snow leopard (*Panthera uncia*)
红外影像：**荒野新疆**
Camera-trap image, Wild Xinjiang
新疆
Xinjiang

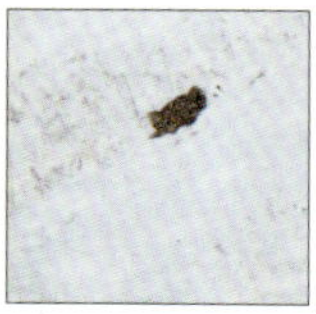

雪豹
Snow leopard (*Panthera uncia*)
杰德·威恩嘉顿　摄
Photo by Jed Weingarten
四川
Sichuan

珠穆朗玛峰
Mount Everest
齐险峰　摄
Photo by Qi Xianfeng
西藏
Tibet

雪豹
Snow leopard (*Panthera uncia*)
林根火　摄
Photo by Lin Genhuo
西藏
Tibet

雪豹
Snow leopard (*Panthera uncia*)
手机拍摄：**卧龙保护区**
Cell phone image, Wolong NR
四川
Sichuan

唐古拉山脉
Tanggula Mountains
谢建国　摄
Photo by Xie Jianguo
青海
Qinghai

塔什库尔干自然保护区，中国最早的雪豹监测工作区
Taxkorgan Nature Reserve, the first snow leopard research site in China
齐险峰　摄
Photo by Qi Xianfeng

雪豹
Snow leopard (*Panthera uncia*)
红外影像：**卧龙保护区**
Camera-trap image, Wolong NR
四川
Sichuan

雪豹
Snow leopard (*Panthera uncia*)
彭建生　摄
Photo by Peng Jiansheng
青海
Qinghai

喜马拉雅旱獭
Himalayan marmot (*Marmota himalayana*)
红外影像：**北京林大**
Camera-trap image, Beijing Forestry University
西藏
Tibet

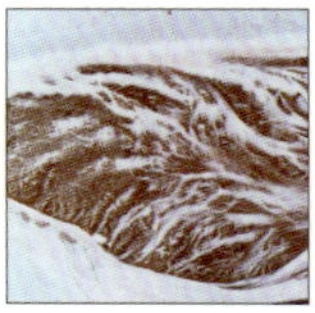

巴颜喀拉山脉
Bayan Kala Mountains
杰德·威恩嘉顿　摄
Photo by Jed Weingarten
青海
Qinghai

雪豹
Snow leopard (*Panthera uncia*)

红外影像：**贡嘎山保护区**
Camera-trap image, Gongga Mountain NR

四川
Sichuan

岩羊
Blue sheep (*Pseudois nayaur*)

冯江 摄
Photo by Feng Jiang

青海
Qinghai

野牦牛
Wild yak (*Bos mutus*)

杰德·威恩嘉顿 摄
Photo by Jed Weingarten

青海
Qinghai

马麝
Alpine musk deer (*Moschus chrysogaster*)

杰德·威恩嘉顿 摄
Photo by Jed Weingarten

四川
Sichuan

雪豹
Snow leopard (*Panthera uncia*)

红外影像：**荒野新疆**
Camera-trap image, Wild Xinjiang

新疆
Xinjiang

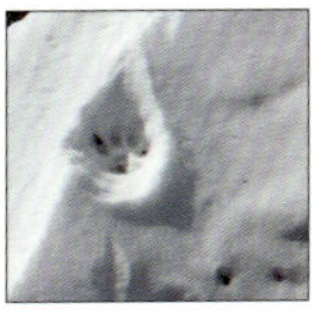

雪豹脚印
The footprint of snow leopard

冯江 摄
Photo by Feng Jiang

青海
Qinghai

雪豹脚印
The footprints of snow leopard

冯江 摄
Photo by Feng Jiang

青海
Qinghai

雪豹
Snow leopard (*Panthera uncia*)

红外影像：**卧龙保护区**
Camera-trap image, Wolong NR

四川
Sichuan

雪豹
Snow leopard (*Panthera uncia*)

红外影像：**荒野新疆**
Camera-trap image, Wild Xinjiang

新疆
Xinjiang

全缘叶绿绒蒿
Entire meconopsis (*Meconopsis integrifolia*)

谢建国 摄
Photo by Xie Jianguo

四川
Sichuan

藏羚羊
Tibetan antelope (*Pantholops hodgsonii*)

杰德·威恩嘉顿 摄
Photo by Jed Weingarten

青海
Qinghai

赤狐
Red fox (*Vulpes vulpes*)

星智 摄
Photo by Xing Zhi

青海
Qinghai

大鵟
Upland buzzard (*Buteo hemilasius*)

徐永春 摄
Photo by Xu Yongchun

青海
Qinghai

黑唇鼠兔
Black-lipped pika (*Ochotona curzoniae*)

徐永春 摄
Photo by Xu Yongchun

青海
Qinghai

雪豹
Snow leopard (*Panthera uncia*)

董磊 摄
Photo by Dong Lei

青海
Qinghai

野牦牛
Wild yak (*Bos mutus*)

杰德·威恩嘉顿 摄
Photo by Jed Weingarten

青海
Qinghai

雪豹脚印
The footprints of snow leopard

冯江 摄
Photo by Feng Jiang

青海
Qinghai

雪豹
Snow leopard (*Panthera uncia*)

红外影像：**盐池湾保护区**
Camera-trap image, Yanchiwan NR

甘肃
Gansu

山丽报春
Beautiful primrose (*Primula bella*)

谢建国 摄
Photo by Xie Jianguo

四川
Sichuan

雪豹
Snow leopard (*Panthera uncia*)

红外影像：**北京林大**
Camera-trap image, Beijing Forestry University

新疆
Xinjiang

金露梅与玛尼石
Bush cinquefoil and Mani Stone

彭建生　摄
Photo by Peng Jiansheng

青海
Qinghai

雪豹
Snow leopard (*Panthera uncia*)

红外影像：卧龙保护区
Camera-trap image, Wolong NR

四川
Sichuan

雪豹
Snow leopard (*Panthera uncia*)

张明　摄
Photo by Zhang Ming

青海
Qinghai

雪豹
Snow leopard (*Panthera uncia*)

三江源保护区　摄
Photo by Sanjiangyuan NR

青海
Qinghai

雪豹
Snow leopard (*Panthera uncia*)

红外影像：贡嘎山保护区
Camera-trap image, Gongga Mountain NR

四川
Sichuan

雪豹
Snow leopard (*Panthera uncia*)

红外影像：贡嘎山保护区
Camera-trap image, Gongga Mountain NR

四川
Sichuan

雪豹
Snow leopard (*Panthera uncia*)

桑布　摄
Photo by Sang Bu

新疆
Xinjiang

雪豹
Snow leopard (*Panthera uncia*)

卧龙保护区　摄
Photo by Wolong NR

四川
Sichuan

雪豹
Snow leopard (*Panthera uncia*)

杰德·威恩嘉顿　摄
Photo by Jed Weingarten

青海
Qinghai

藏原羚
Tibetan gazelle (*Procapra picticaudata*)

冯江　摄
Photo by Feng Jiang

青海
Qinghai

多刺绿绒蒿
Spiny meconopsis (*Meconopsis horridula*)

彭建生　摄
Photo by Peng Jiansheng

青海
Qinghai

雪豹
Snow leopard (*Panthera uncia*)

红外影像：三江源保护区
Camera-trap image, Sanjiangyuan NR

青海
Qinghai

雪豹
Snow leopard (*Panthera uncia*)

红外影像：三江源保护区
Camera-trap image, Sanjiangyuan NR

青海
Qinghai

雪豹
Snow leopard (*Panthera uncia*)

杰德·威恩嘉顿　摄
Photo by Jed Weingarten

四川
Sichuan

雪豹
Snow leopard (*Panthera uncia*)

杰德·威恩嘉顿　摄
Photo by Jed Weingarten

四川
Sichuan

雪豹
Snow leopard (*Panthera uncia*)

杰德·威恩嘉顿　摄
Photo by Jed Weingarten

四川
Sichuan

雪豹
Snow leopard (*Panthera uncia*)

杰德·威恩嘉顿　摄
Photo by Jed Weingarten

青海
Qinghai

雪豹
Snow leopard (*Panthera uncia*)

红外影像：盐池湾保护区
Camera-trap image, Yanchiwan NR

甘肃
Gansu

雪豹
Snow leopard (*Panthera uncia*)

杰德·威恩嘉顿　摄
Photo by Jed Weingarten

青海
Qinghai

高山兀鹫
Himalayan griffon vulture (*Gyps himalayensis*)

冯江　摄
Photo by Feng Jiang

青海
Qinghai

野牦牛
Wild yak (*Bos mutus*)

星智　摄
Photo by Xing Zhi

青海
Qinghai

雪豹
Snow leopard (*Panthera uncia*)

董磊　摄
Photo by Dong Lei

青海
Qinghai

雪豹
Snow leopard (*Panthera uncia*)

红外影像：**三江源保护区**
Camera-trap image, Sanjiangyuan NR

青海
Qinghai

雪豹
Snow leopard (*Panthera uncia*)

红外影像：**祁连山保护区**
Camera-trap image, Qilian Mountain NR

青海
Qinghai

雪豹
Snow leopard (*Panthera uncia*)

红外影像：**盐池湾保护区**
Camera-trap image, Yanchiwan NR

甘肃
Gansu

雪豹
Snow leopard (*Panthera uncia*)

红外影像：**卧龙保护区**
Camera-trap image, Wolong NR

四川
Sichuan

雪豹
Snow leopard (*Panthera uncia*)

红外影像：**北京林大**
Camera-trap image, Beijing Forestry University

新疆
Xinjiang

雪豹
Snow leopard (*Panthera uncia*)

红外影像：**北京林大**
Camera-trap image, Beijing Forestry University

西藏
Tibet

雪豹
Snow leopard (*Panthera uncia*)

张明　摄
Photo by Zhang Ming

青海
Qinghai

雪豹
Snow leopard (*Panthera uncia*)

红外影像：**卧龙保护区**
Camera-trap image, Wolong NR

四川
Sichuan

雪豹
Snow leopard (*Panthera uncia*)

红外影像：**卧龙保护区**
Camera-trap image, Wolong NR

四川
Sichuan

雪豹
Snow leopard (*Panthera uncia*)

红外影像：**新龙县环林局**
Camera-trap image, Xinlong Forestry Bureau

四川
Qinghai

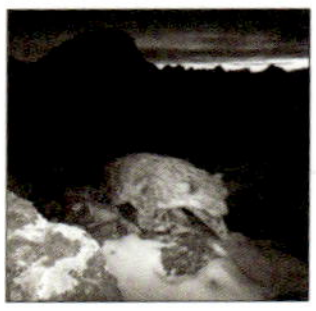

雪豹
Snow leopard (*Panthera uncia*)

红外影像：**卧龙保护区**
Camera-trap image, Wolong NR

四川
Sichuan

雪豹
Snow leopard (*Panthera uncia*)

林根火　摄
Photo by Lin Genhuo

西藏
Tibet

雪豹
Snow leopard (*Panthera uncia*)

杰德·威恩嘉顿　摄
Photo by Jed Weingarten

四川
Sichuan

雪豹
Snow leopard (*Panthera uncia*)

阿拉善森林公安　摄
Photo by Alashan Forest Public Security

内蒙古
Inner Mongolia

雪豹
Snow leopard (*Panthera uncia*)

杰德·威恩嘉顿　摄
Photo by Jed Weingarten

青海
Qinghai

雪豹
Snow leopard (*Panthera uncia*)

杰德·威恩嘉顿　摄
Photo by Jed Weingarten

四川
Sichuan

雪豹
Snow leopard (*Panthera uncia*)

红外影像：**荒野新疆**
Camera-trap image, Wild Xinjiang

新疆
Xinjiang

唐古特雪莲
Snow lotus (*Saussurea tangutica*)

彭建生　摄
Photo by Peng Jiansheng

青海
Qinghai

雪豹
Snow leopard (*Panthera uncia*)

红外影像：**三江源保护区**
Camera-trap image, Sanjiangyuan NR

青海
Qinghai

雪豹
Snow leopard (*Panthera uncia*)

红外影像：**盐池湾保护区**
Camera-trap image, Yanchiwan NR

甘肃
Gansu

雪豹
Snow leopard (*Panthera uncia*)

杰德·威恩嘉顿 摄
Photo by Jed Weingarten

四川
Sichuan

藏狐
Tibetan fox (*Vulpes ferrilata*)

谢建国 摄
Photo by Xie Jianguo

青海
Qinghai

昆仑山谷
Valley of Kunlun Mountains

斯塔凡·威斯特兰德 摄
Photo by Staffan Widstrand

青海
Qinghai

雪豹
Snow leopard (*Panthera uncia*)

林根火 摄
Photo by Lin Genhuo

西藏
Tibet

被救助的雪豹
The rescued snow leopard

谢建国 摄
Photo by Xie Jianguo

青海
Qinghai

雪豹
Snow leopard (*Panthera uncia*)

红外影像：**北京林大**
Camera-trap image, Beijing Forestry University

新疆
Xinjiang

野外巡护
Field patrol

鞍子河保护区 摄
Photo by Anzihe NR

四川
Sichuan

雪豹
Snow leopard (*Panthera uncia*)

初雯雯 摄
Photo by Chu Wenwen

新疆
Xinjiang

雪豹
Snow leopard (*Panthera uncia*)

彭建生 摄
Photo by Peng Jiansheng

青海
Qinghai

青藏高原
Tibetan Plateau

彭建生 摄
Photo by Peng Jiansheng

祁连山脉
Qilian Mountains

盐池湾保护区 摄
Photo by Yanchiwan NR

甘肃
Gansu

雪豹
Snow leopard (*Panthera uncia*)

张明 摄
Photo by Zhang Ming

青海
Qinghai

赤狐
Red fox (*Vulpes vulpes*)

谢建国 摄
Photo by Xie Jianguo

青海
Qinghai

雪豹
Snow leopard (*Panthera uncia*)

红外影像：**卧龙保护区**
Camera-trap image, Wolong NR

四川
Sichuan

雪豹
Snow leopard (*Panthera uncia*)

桑布 摄
Photo by Sang Bu

新疆
Xinjiang

雪豹调研
Investigating the snow leopard

卧龙保护区 摄
Photo by Wolong NR

四川
Sichuan

图书在版编目(CIP)数据

我，雪豹……：手书·彩图·中英文版 / 吉狄马加著；（美）梅丹理（Denis Mair）译．-- 郑州：河南科学技术出版社，2018.12

ISBN 978-7-5349-9403-6

Ⅰ．①我… Ⅱ．①吉… ②梅… Ⅲ．①诗集—中国—当代 Ⅳ．①I227

中国版本图书馆 CIP 数据核字（2018）第 271665 号

出版发行：河南科学技术出版社

地址：郑州市金水东路 39 号　　邮编：450016

电话：（0371）65788673　65788110

网址：www.hnstp.cn

图书策划：何向阳　李喜婷

图片策划：谢建国　徐永春

科学顾问：尹　峰

责任编辑：汪林中

英文编辑：李喜婷

责任校对：于凯燕

装帧设计：视觉共振设计工作室 010-62015184 774038217@QQ.COM

封面摄影：谢建国

责任印制：张　巍

印　　刷：北京盛通印刷股份有限公司

经　　销：全国新华书店

开　　本：889 mm×1 194 mm　1/16

印　　张：10　　字数：320 千字

版　　次：2018 年 12 月第 1 版　2018 年 12 月第 1 次印刷

定　　价：88.00 元